P9-CBG-720

SUPER POTATO

#6 SUPER POTATO GETS BUFF

ARTUR LAPERLA

Graphic Universe™ • Minneapolis

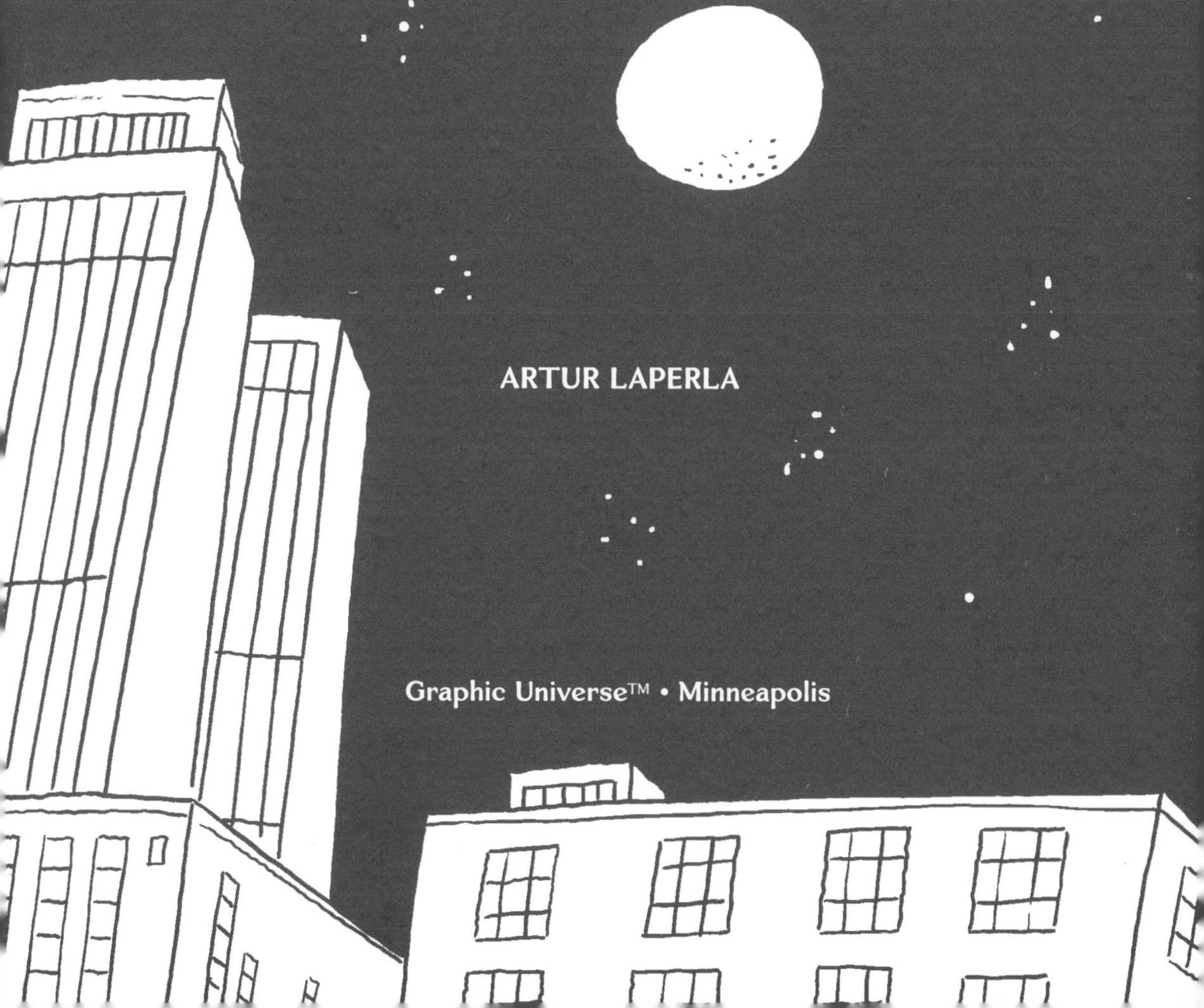

Story and illustrations by Artur Laperla
Translation by Norwyn MacTíre

First American edition published in 2021 by Graphic Universe™

Copyright © 2017 by Artur Laperla and Bang. Ediciones. Published by arrangement with Garbuix Agency.

Graphic Universe™ is a trademark of Lerner Publishing Group, Inc.

Graphic Universe™
An imprint of Lerner Publishing Group, Inc.
241 First Avenue North
Minneapolis, MN 55401 USA

For reading levels and more information, look up this title at www.lernerbooks.com.

Main body text set in CCWildWords. Typeface provided by Comicraft.

Library of Congress Cataloging-in-Publication Data

Names: Laperla (Artist), author, illustrator. | MacTire, Norwyn, translator.
Title: Super Potato gets buff / Artur Laperla ; translation by Norwyn MacTíre.
Other titles: Super Patata. 6. English
Description: First American edition. | Minneapolis, MN : Graphic Universe, 2021. | Series: Super Potato book 6 | Audience: Ages 7–11 | Audience: Grades 2–3 | Summary: "Gigantic flies are rampaging at a research center, thanks to a beam that boosted their molecules! Fortunately, the beam also creates a gigantic Super Potato . . . who's delighted with his new muscles" —Provided by publisher.
Identifiers: LCCN 2020006429 (print) | LCCN 2020006430 (ebook) | ISBN 9781512440263 (library binding) | ISBN 9781728417523 (ebook)
Subjects: LCSH: Graphic novels. | CYAC: Graphic novels. | Superheroes—Fiction. | Potatoes—Fiction. | Humorous stories.
Classification: LCC PZ7.7.L367 Sv 2020 (print) | LCC PZ7.7.L367 (ebook) | DDC 741.5/973—dc23

LC record available at https://lccn.loc.gov/2020006429
LC ebook record available at https://lccn.loc.gov/2020006430

Manufactured in the United States of America
1-42295-26145-6/10/2020

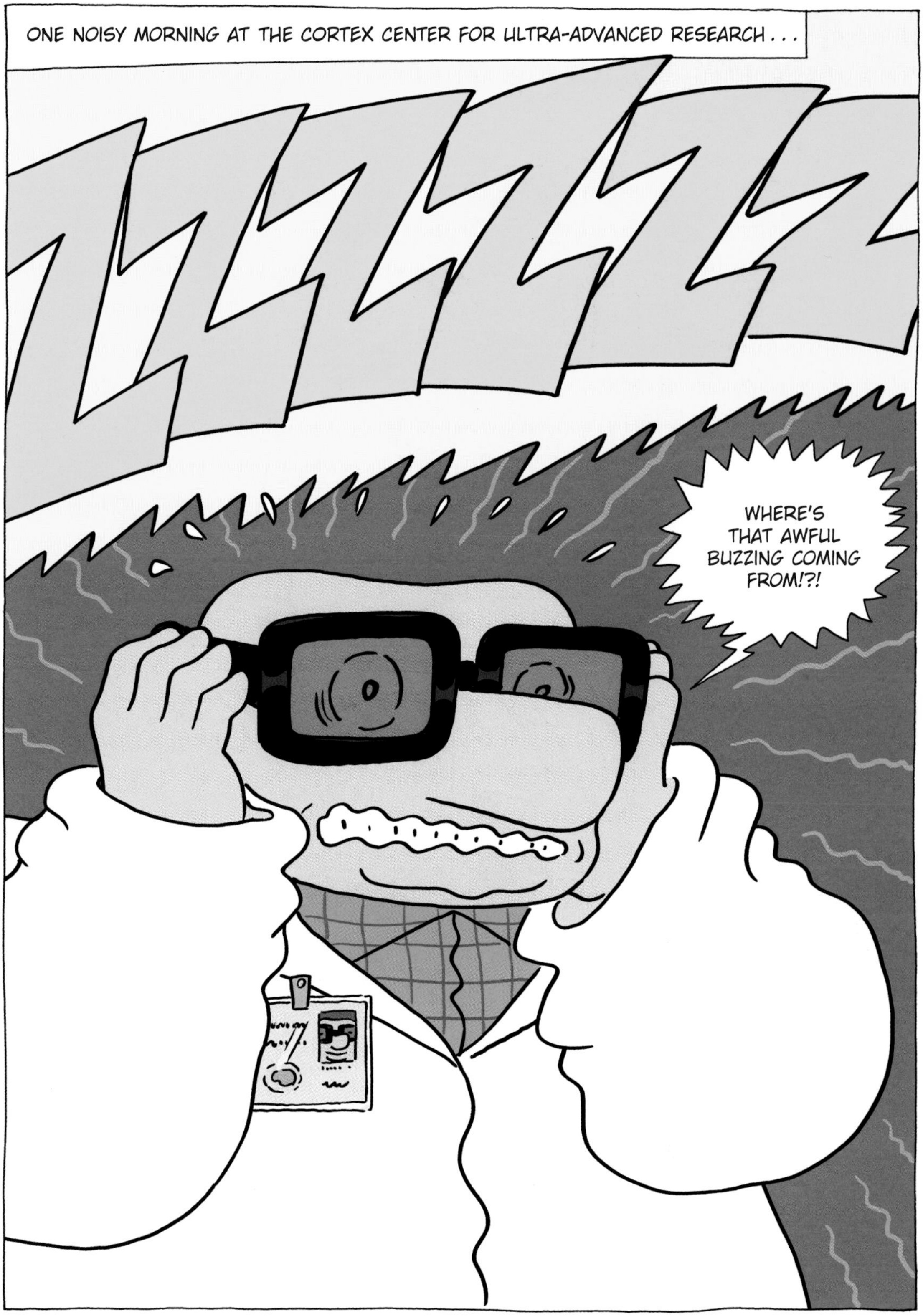
ONE NOISY MORNING AT THE CORTEX CENTER FOR ULTRA-ADVANCED RESEARCH . . .
ZZZZZZ
WHERE'S THAT AWFUL BUZZING COMING FROM!?!

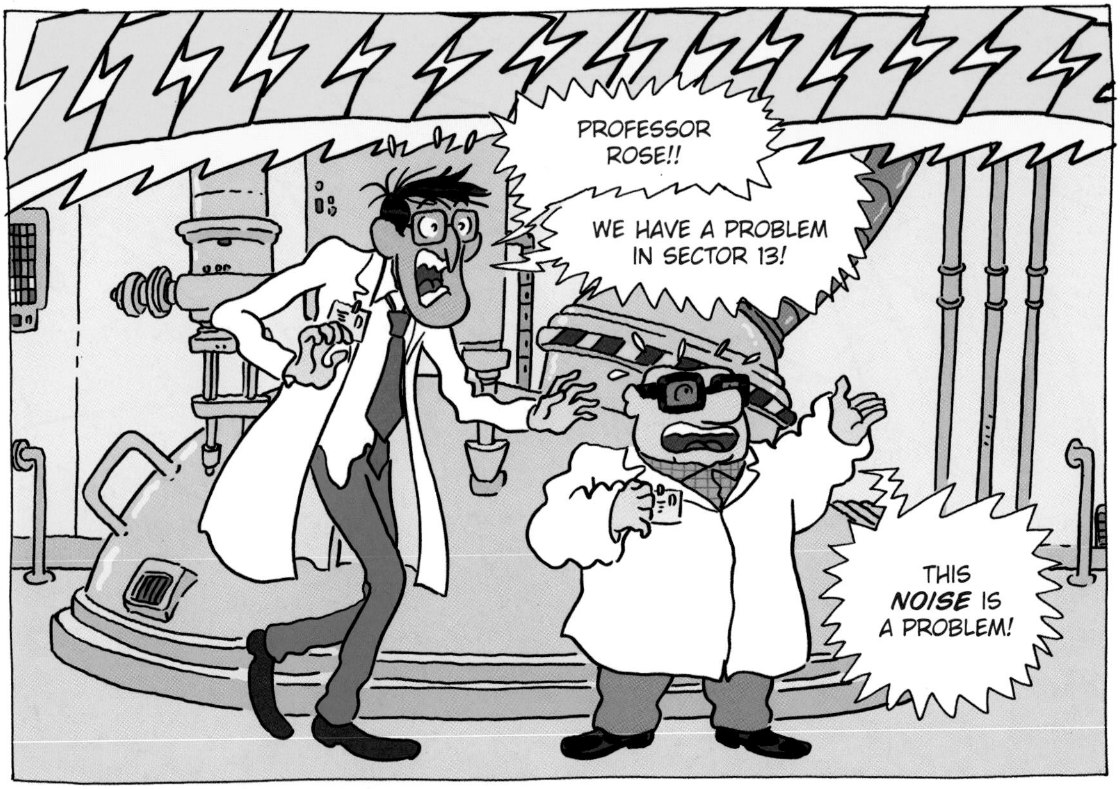
PROFESSOR ROSE!!
WE HAVE A PROBLEM IN SECTOR 13!
THIS NOISE IS A PROBLEM!

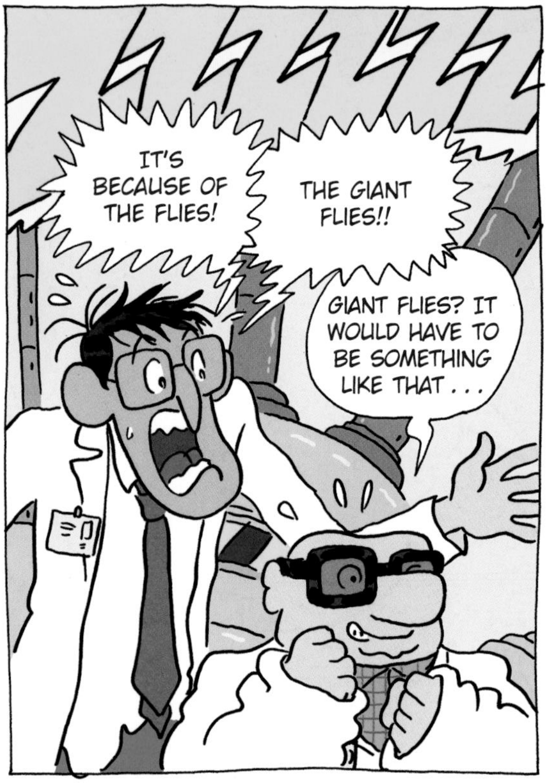
IT'S BECAUSE OF THE FLIES!
THE GIANT FLIES!!
GIANT FLIES? IT WOULD HAVE TO BE SOMETHING LIKE THAT . . .

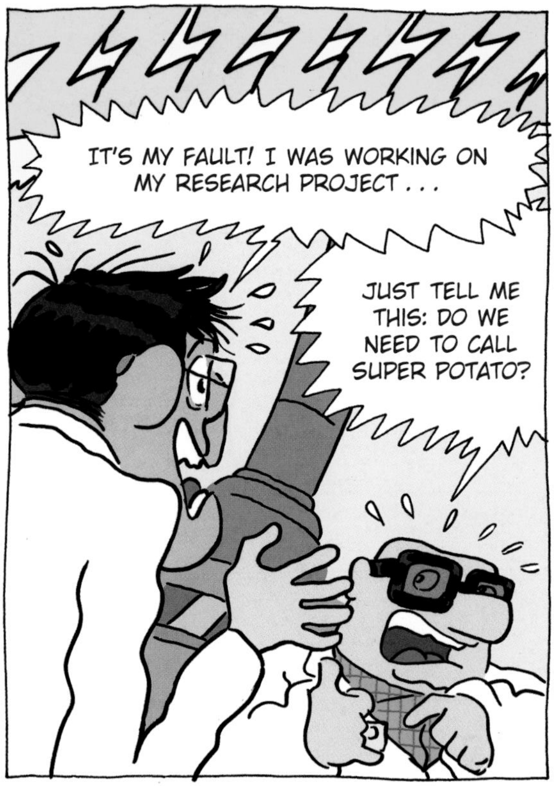
IT'S MY FAULT! I WAS WORKING ON MY RESEARCH PROJECT . . .
JUST TELL ME THIS: DO WE NEED TO CALL SUPER POTATO?

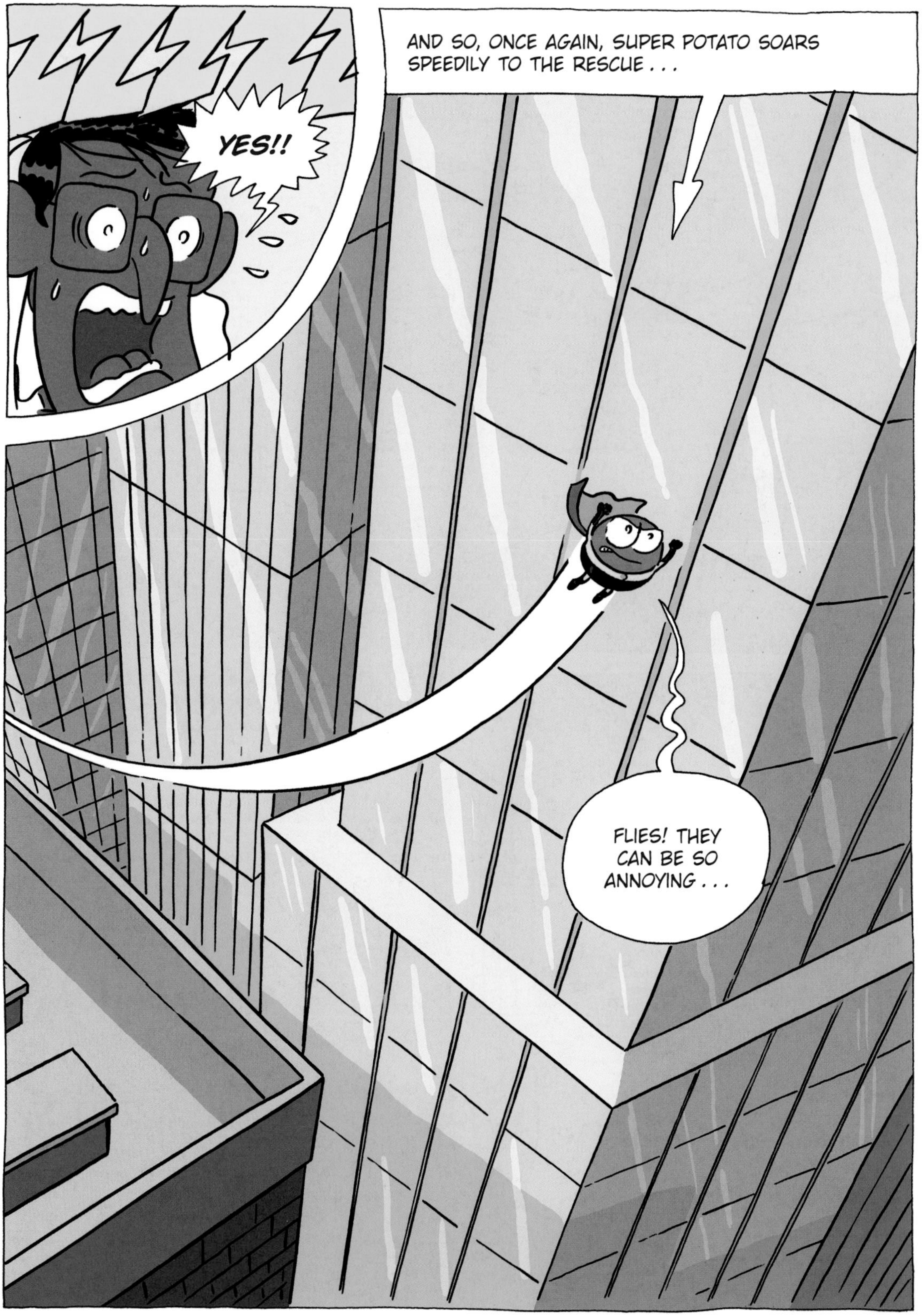
YES!!
AND SO, ONCE AGAIN, SUPER POTATO SOARS SPEEDILY TO THE RESCUE . . .
FLIES! THEY CAN BE SO ANNOYING . . .

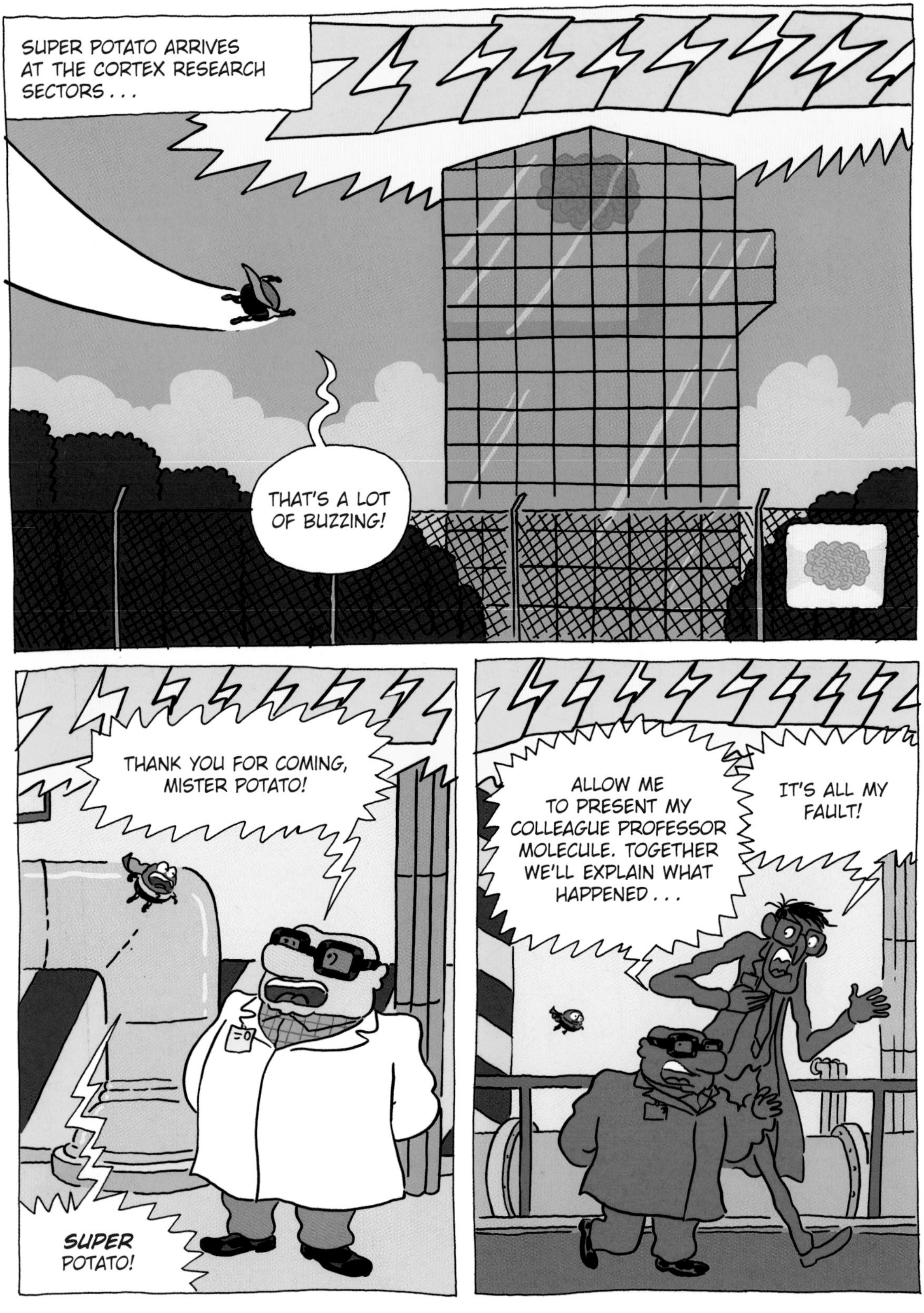
SUPER POTATO ARRIVES AT THE CORTEX RESEARCH SECTORS . . .
THAT'S A LOT OF BUZZING!
THANK YOU FOR COMING, MISTER POTATO!
SUPER POTATO!
ALLOW ME TO PRESENT MY COLLEAGUE PROFESSOR MOLECULE. TOGETHER WE'LL EXPLAIN WHAT HAPPENED . . .
IT'S ALL MY FAULT!

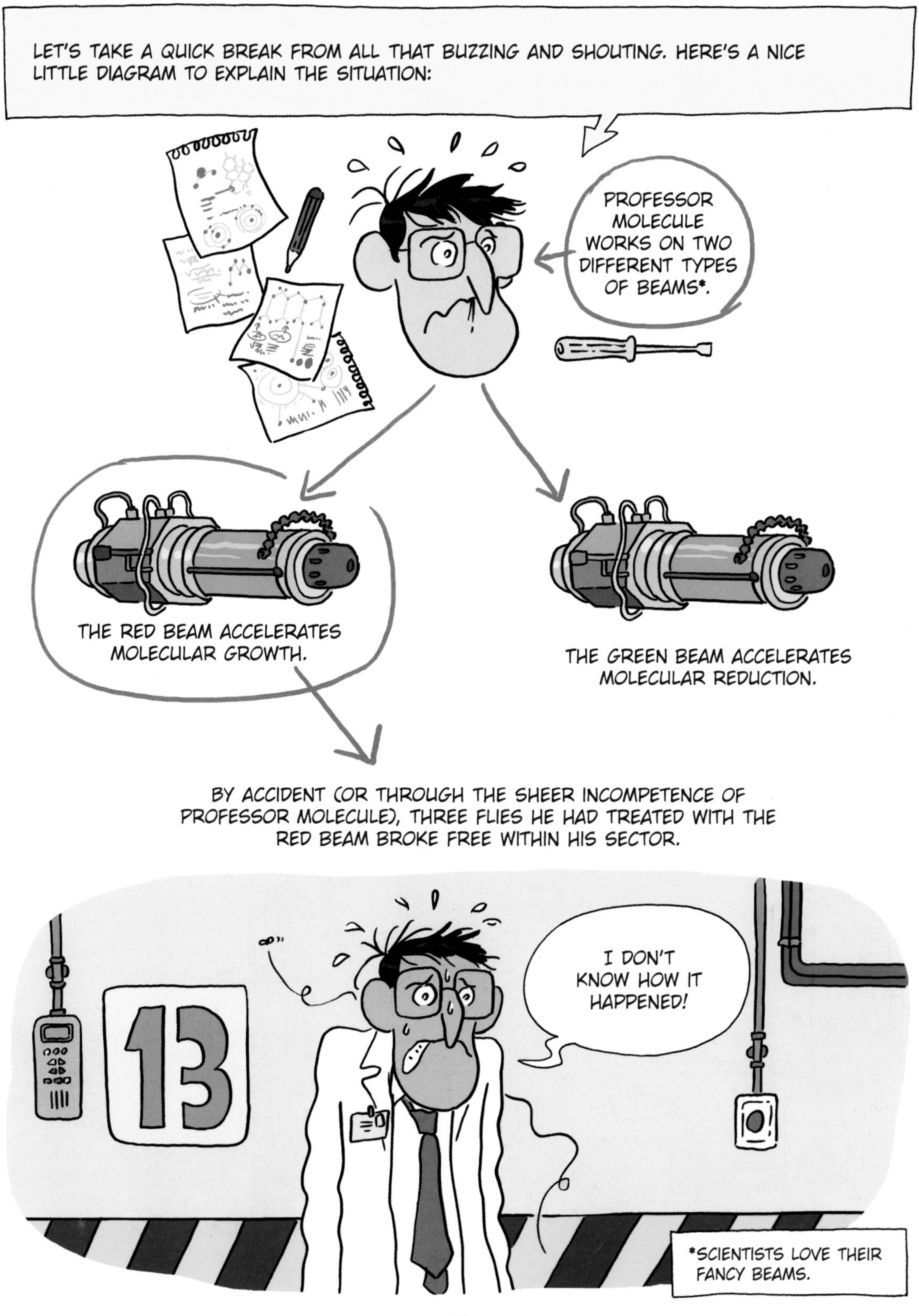
LET'S TAKE A QUICK BREAK FROM ALL THAT BUZZING AND SHOUTING. HERE'S A NICE LITTLE DIAGRAM TO EXPLAIN THE SITUATION:
PROFESSOR MOLECULE WORKS ON TWO DIFFERENT TYPES OF BEAMS*.
THE RED BEAM ACCELERATES MOLECULAR GROWTH.
THE GREEN BEAM ACCELERATES MOLECULAR REDUCTION.
BY ACCIDENT (OR THROUGH THE SHEER INCOMPETENCE OF PROFESSOR MOLECULE), THREE FLIES HE HAD TREATED WITH THE RED BEAM BROKE FREE WITHIN HIS SECTOR.
13
I DON'T KNOW HOW IT HAPPENED!
*SCIENTISTS LOVE THEIR FANCY BEAMS.

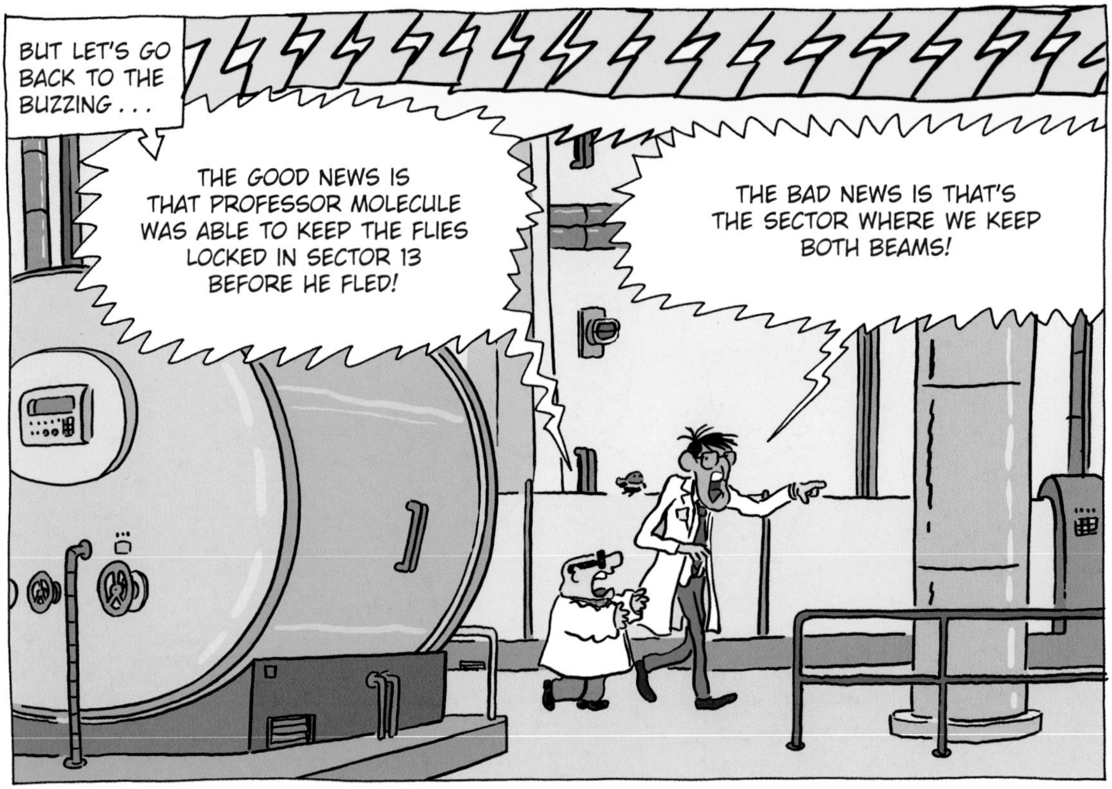
BUT LET'S GO BACK TO THE BUZZING . . .
THE GOOD NEWS IS THAT PROFESSOR MOLECULE WAS ABLE TO KEEP THE FLIES LOCKED IN SECTOR 13 BEFORE HE FLED!
THE BAD NEWS IS THAT'S THE SECTOR WHERE WE KEEP BOTH BEAMS!

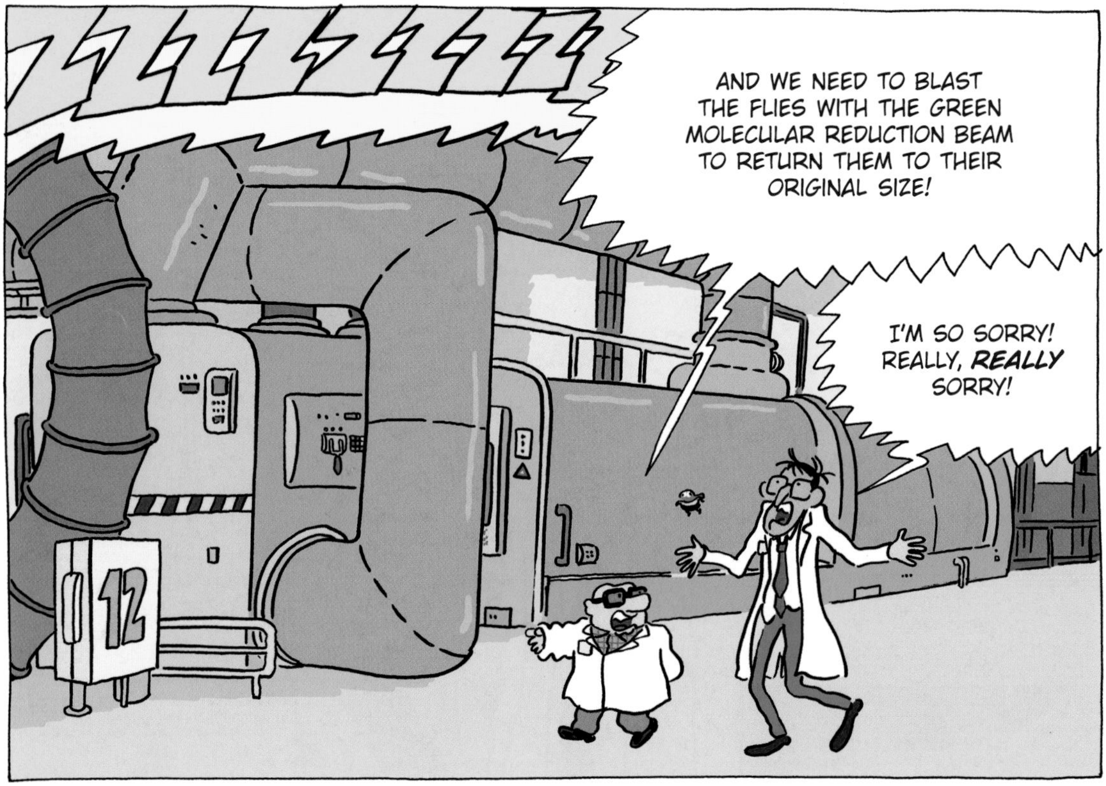
AND WE NEED TO BLAST THE FLIES WITH THE GREEN MOLECULAR REDUCTION BEAM TO RETURN THEM TO THEIR ORIGINAL SIZE!
I'M SO SORRY! REALLY, ***REALLY*** SORRY!
12

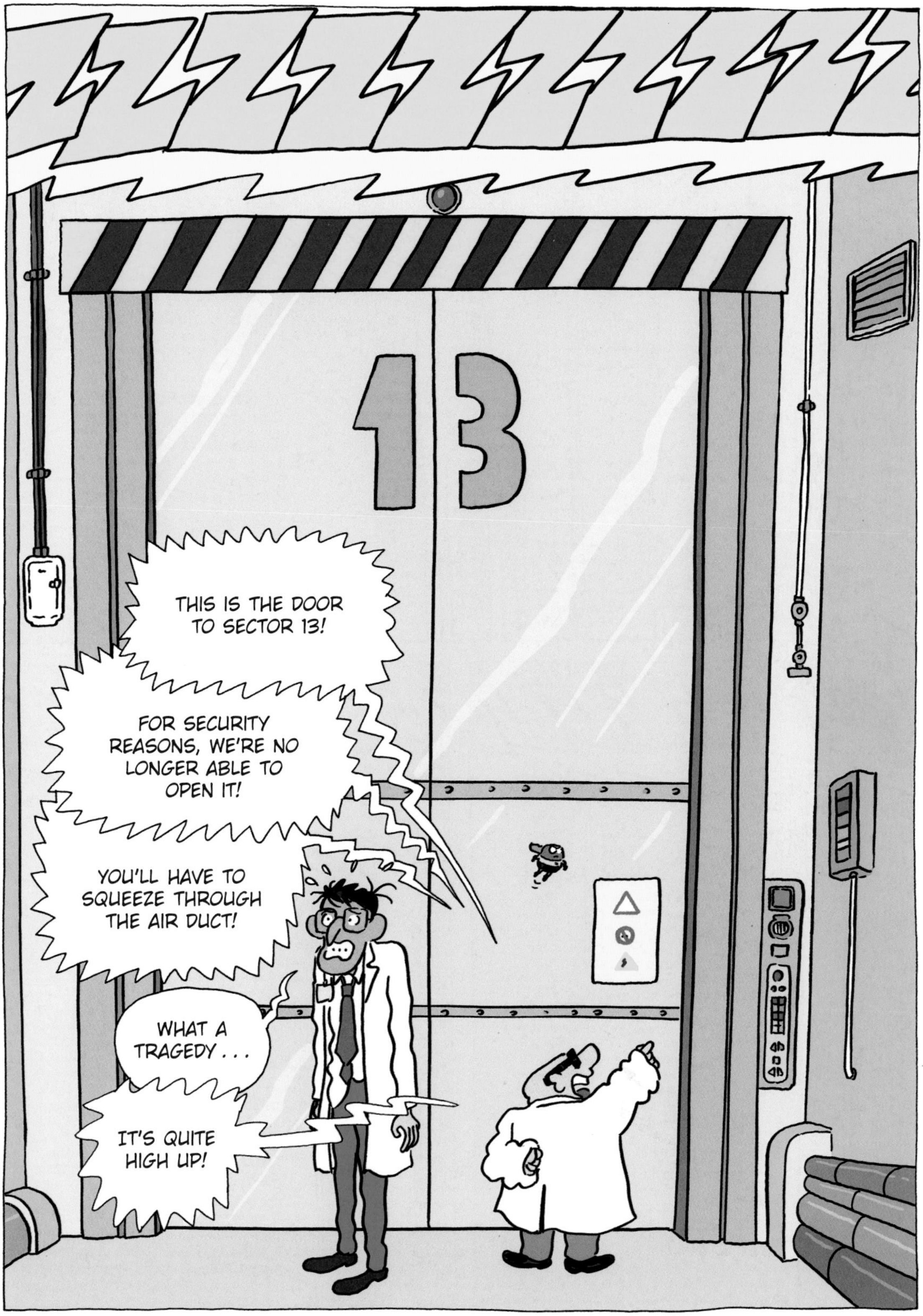
THIS IS THE DOOR TO SECTOR 13!
FOR SECURITY REASONS, WE'RE NO LONGER ABLE TO OPEN IT!
YOU'LL HAVE TO SQUEEZE THROUGH THE AIR DUCT!
WHAT A TRAGEDY . . .
IT'S QUITE HIGH UP!
13

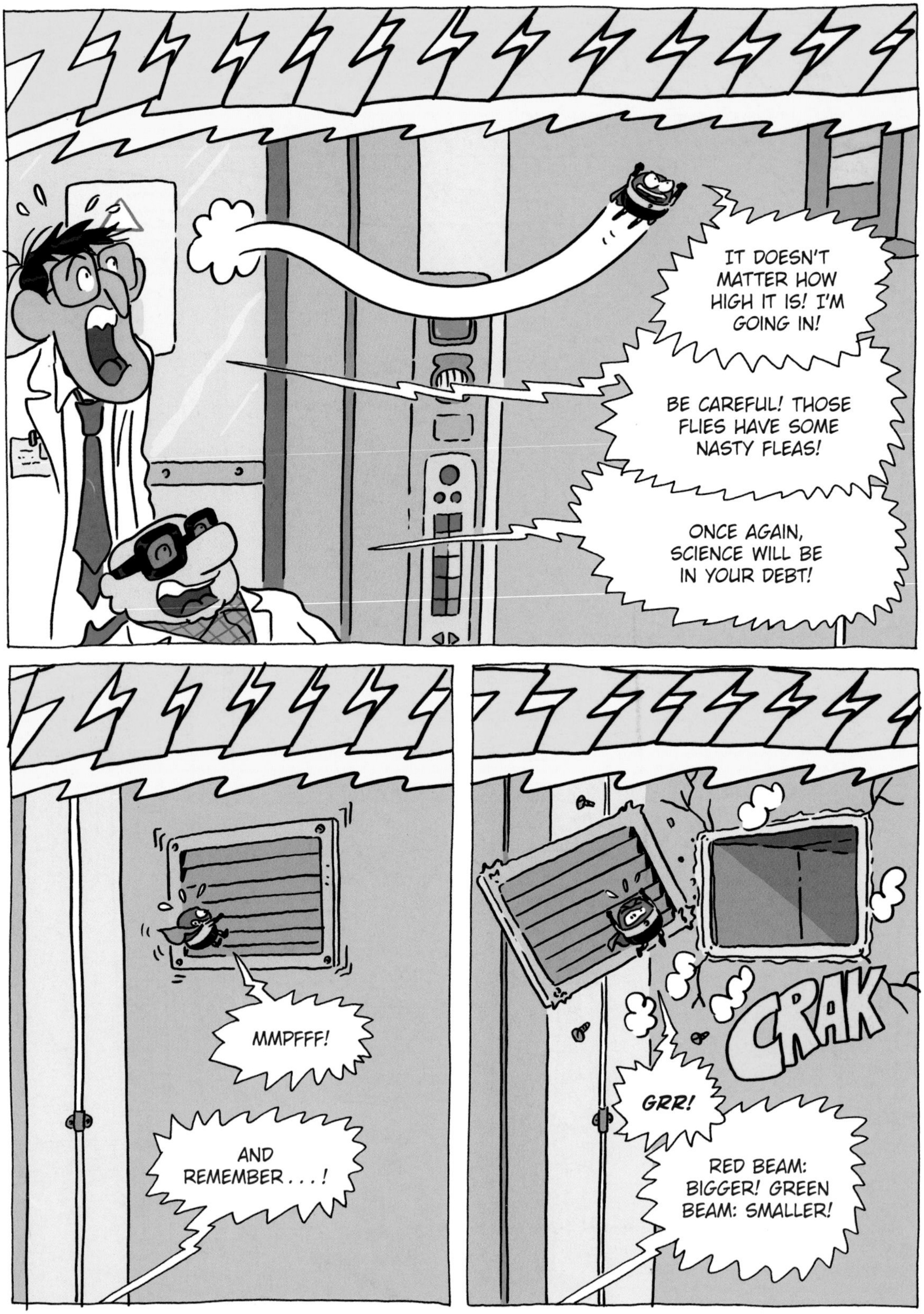

IT DOESN'T MATTER HOW HIGH IT IS! I'M GOING IN!
BE CAREFUL! THOSE FLIES HAVE SOME NASTY FLEAS!
ONCE AGAIN, SCIENCE WILL BE IN YOUR DEBT!
MMPFFF!
AND REMEMBER . . . !
CRAK
GRR!
RED BEAM: BIGGER! GREEN BEAM: SMALLER!

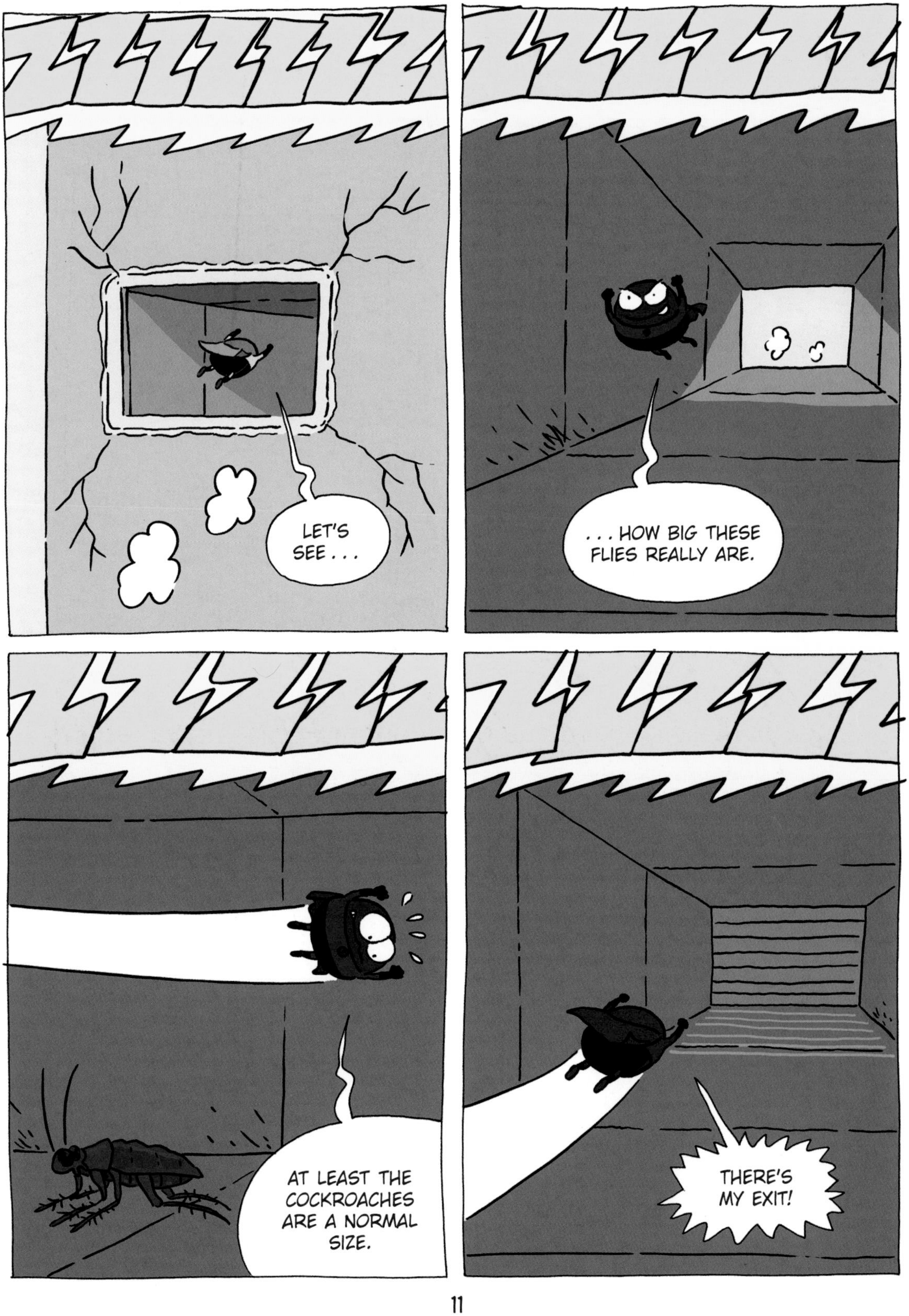
LET'S SEE . . .
. . . HOW BIG THESE FLIES REALLY ARE.
AT LEAST THE COCKROACHES ARE A NORMAL SIZE.
THERE'S MY EXIT!

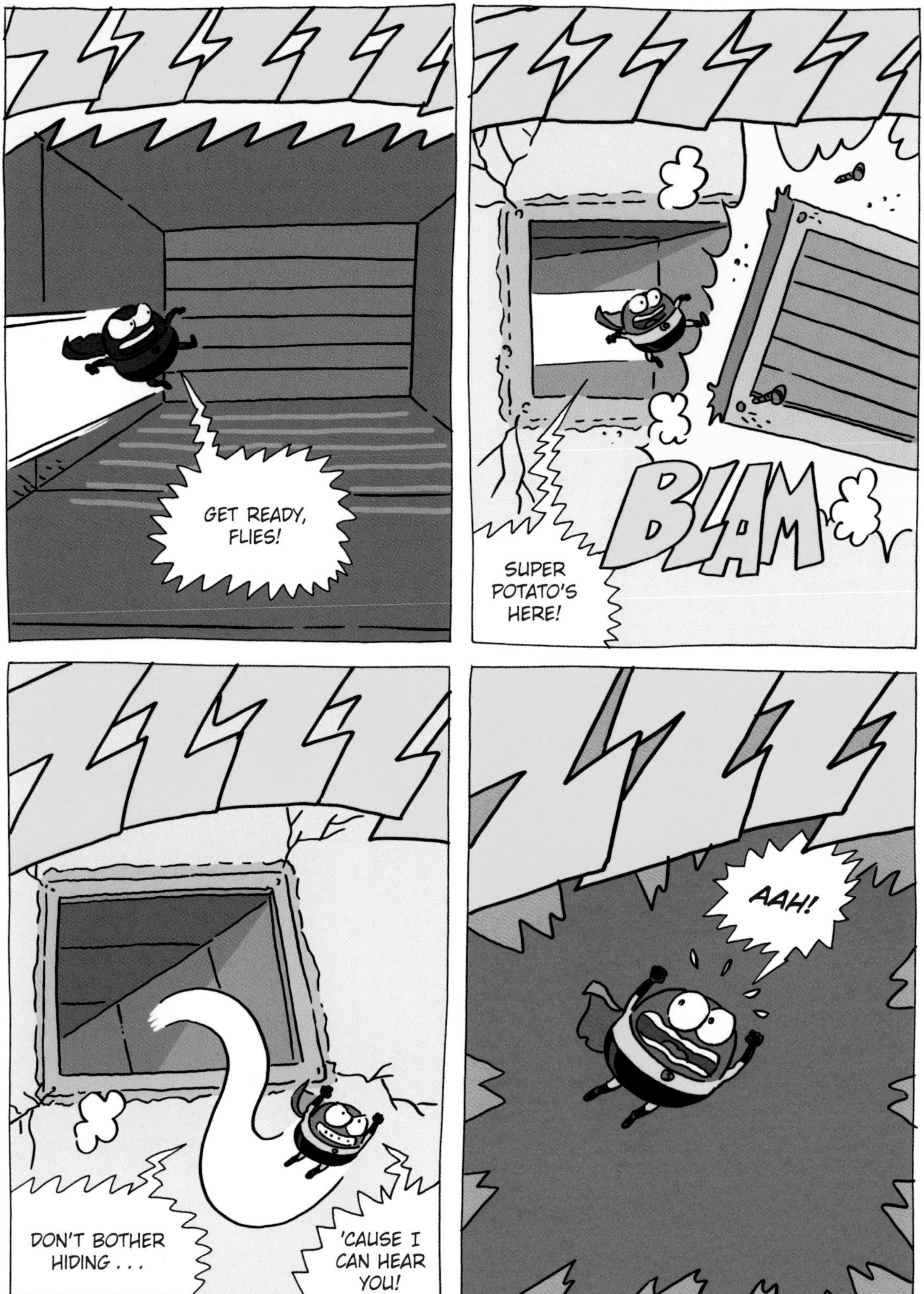
GET READY, FLIES!
SUPER POTATO'S HERE!
BLAM
DON'T BOTHER HIDING . . .
'CAUSE I CAN HEAR YOU!
AAH!

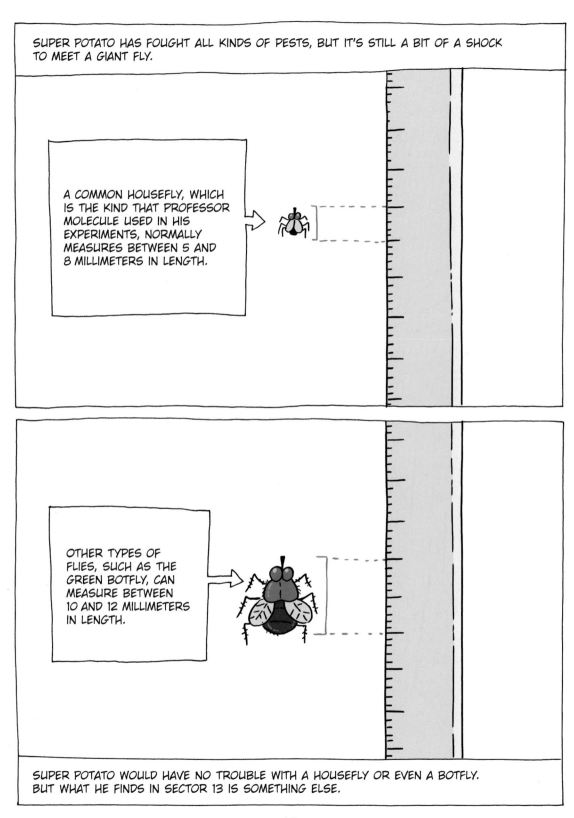

SUPER POTATO HAS FOUGHT ALL KINDS OF PESTS, BUT IT'S STILL A BIT OF A SHOCK TO MEET A GIANT FLY.

A COMMON HOUSEFLY, WHICH IS THE KIND THAT PROFESSOR MOLECULE USED IN HIS EXPERIMENTS, NORMALLY MEASURES BETWEEN 5 AND 8 MILLIMETERS IN LENGTH.

OTHER TYPES OF FLIES, SUCH AS THE GREEN BOTFLY, CAN MEASURE BETWEEN 10 AND 12 MILLIMETERS IN LENGTH.

SUPER POTATO WOULD HAVE NO TROUBLE WITH A HOUSEFLY OR EVEN A BOTFLY. BUT WHAT HE FINDS IN SECTOR 13 IS SOMETHING ELSE.

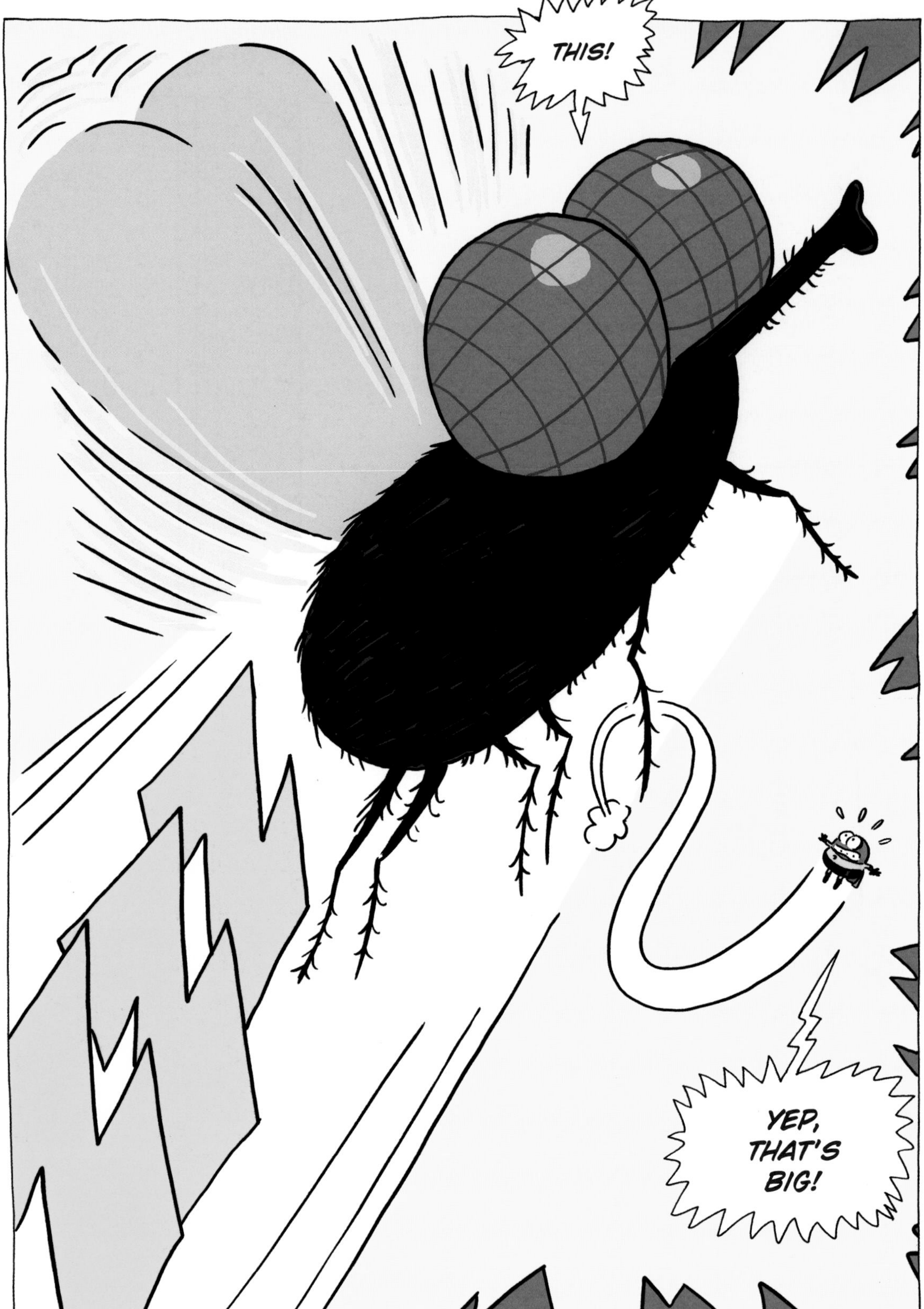
THIS!
YEP, THAT'S BIG!

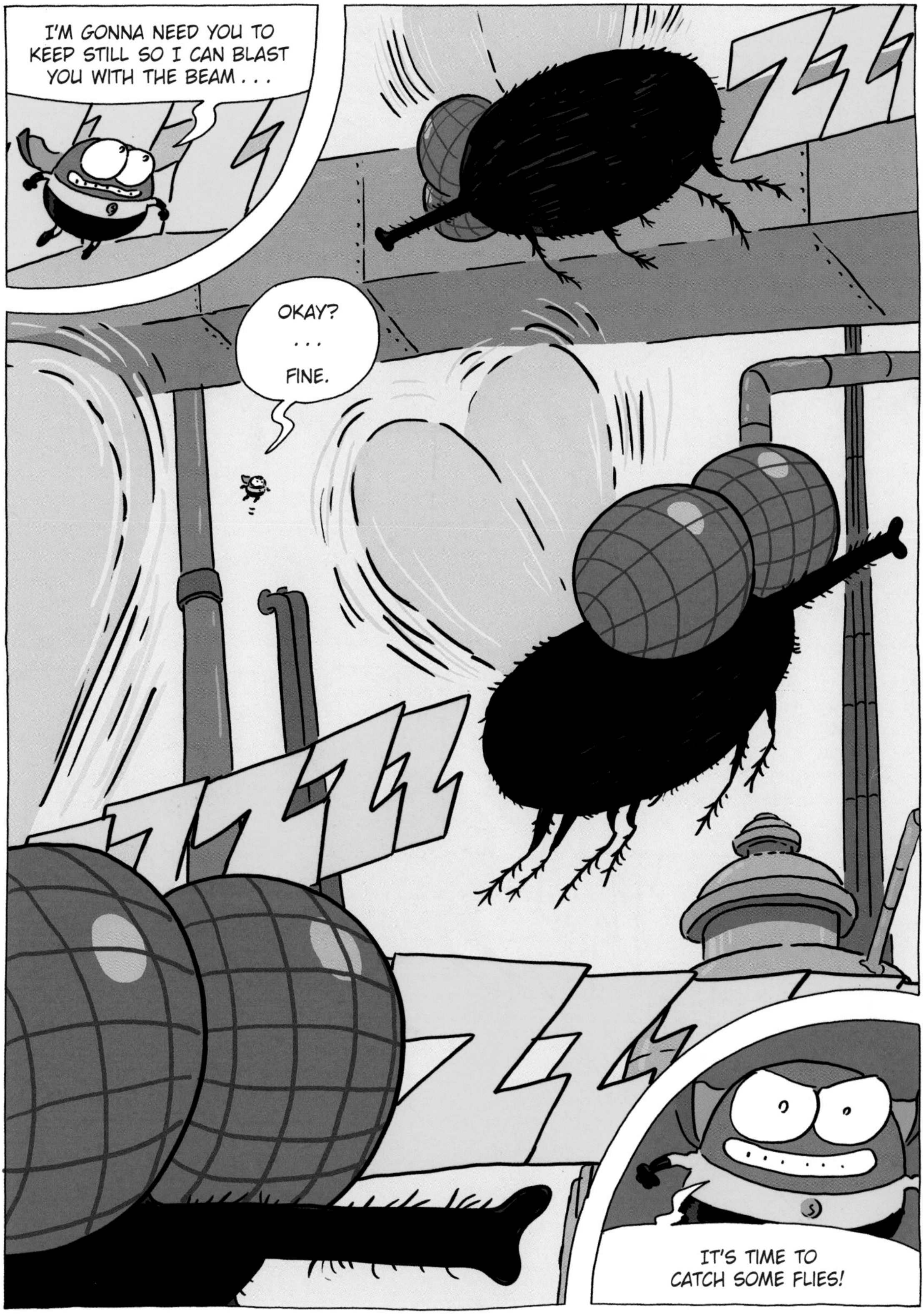
I'M GONNA NEED YOU TO KEEP STILL SO I CAN BLAST YOU WITH THE BEAM . . .
OKAY?
. . .
FINE.
IT'S TIME TO CATCH SOME FLIES!

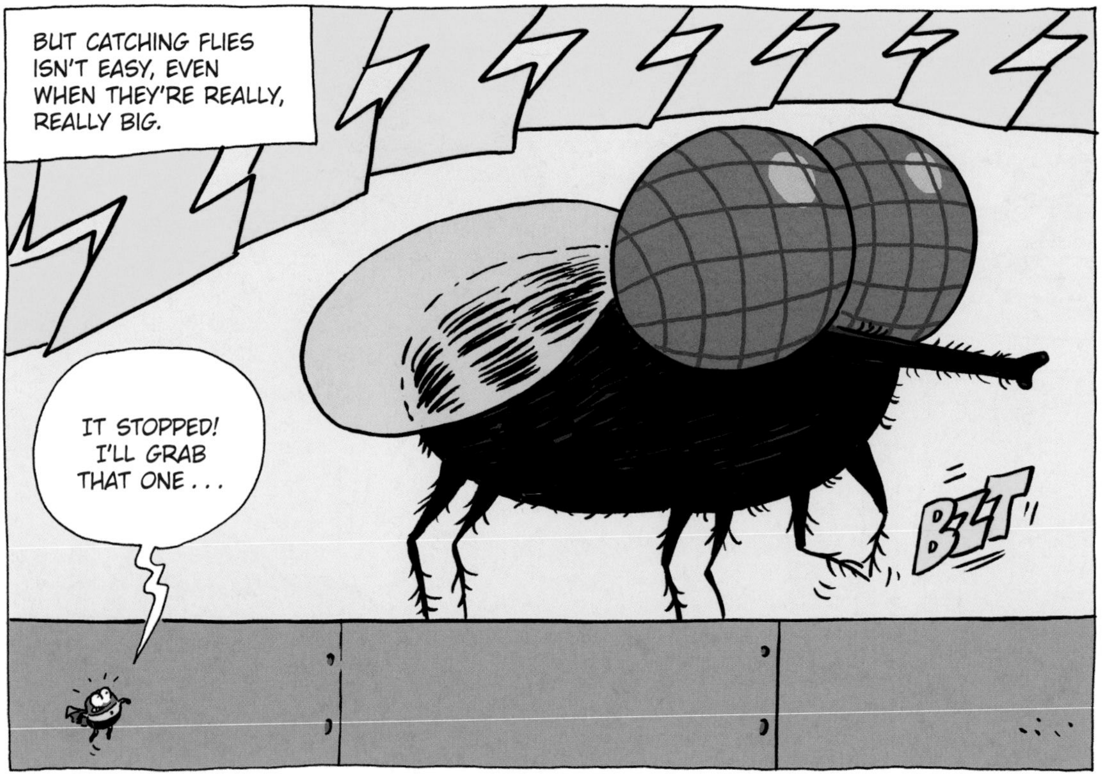
BUT CATCHING FLIES ISN'T EASY, EVEN WHEN THEY'RE REALLY, REALLY BIG.
IT STOPPED! I'LL GRAB THAT ONE . . .
BZZT

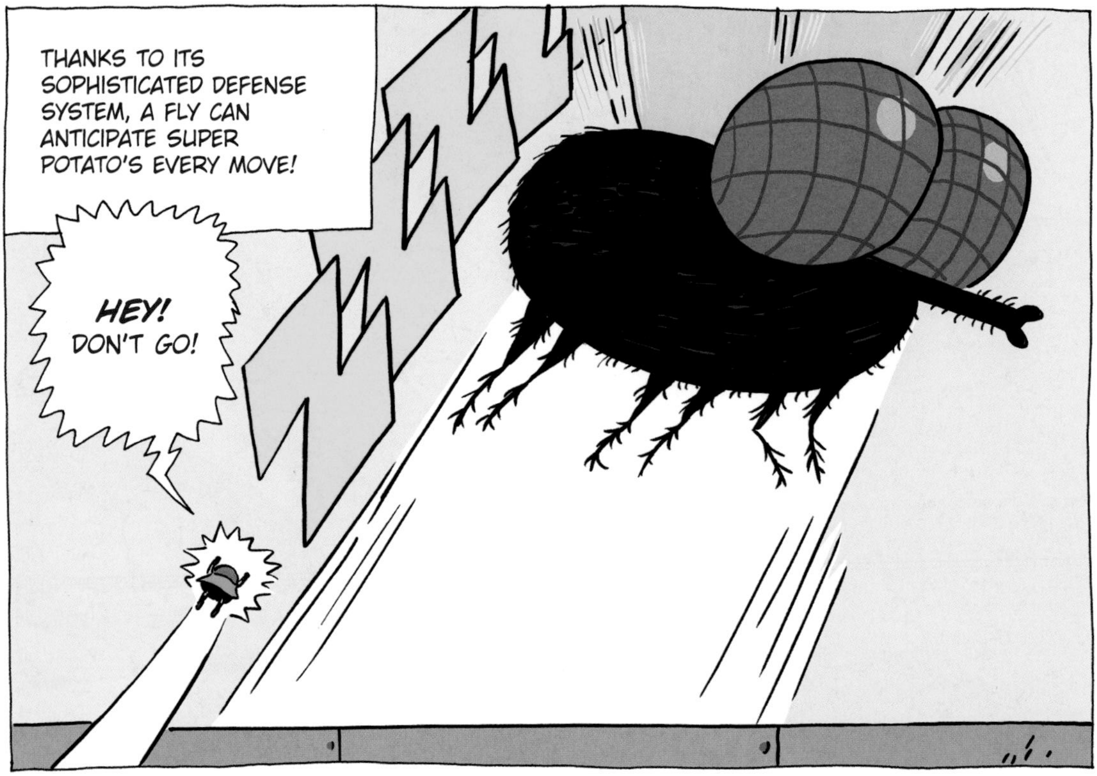
THANKS TO ITS SOPHISTICATED DEFENSE SYSTEM, A FLY CAN ANTICIPATE SUPER POTATO'S EVERY MOVE!
HEY! DON'T GO!

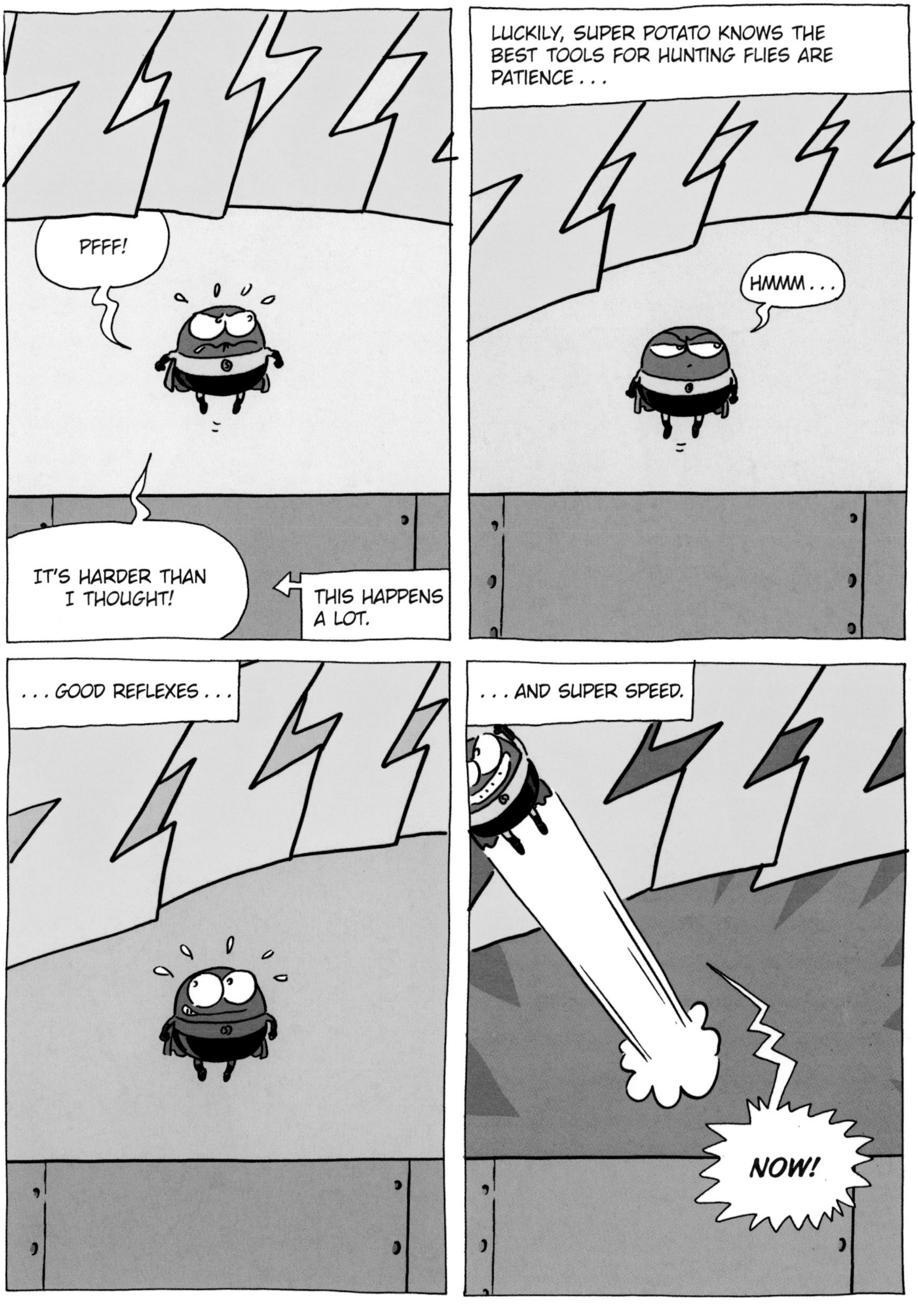
PFFF!
IT'S HARDER THAN I THOUGHT!
THIS HAPPENS A LOT.
LUCKILY, SUPER POTATO KNOWS THE BEST TOOLS FOR HUNTING FLIES ARE PATIENCE . . .
HMMM . . .
. . . GOOD REFLEXES . . .
. . . AND SUPER SPEED.
NOW!

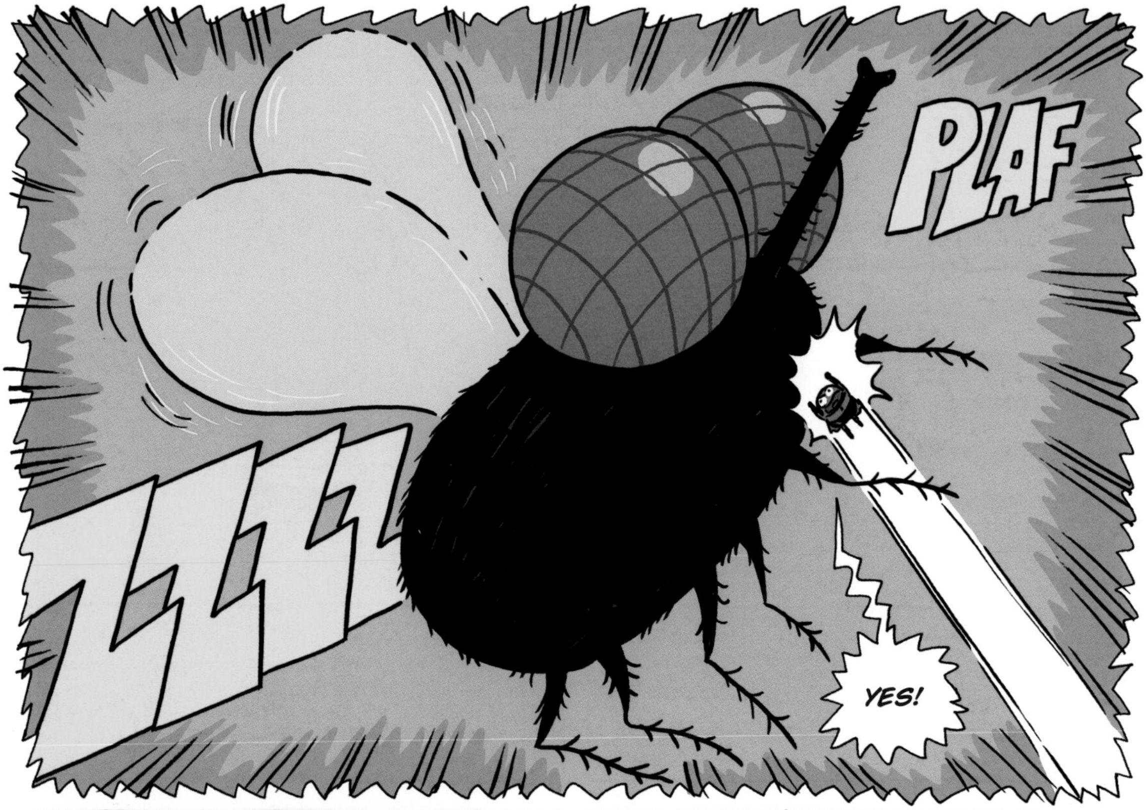
PLAF
YES!

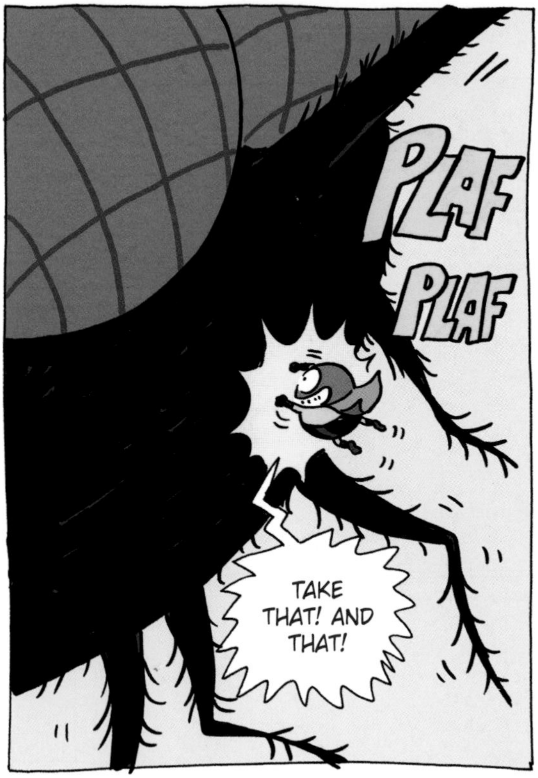
PLAF
PLAF
TAKE THAT! AND THAT!

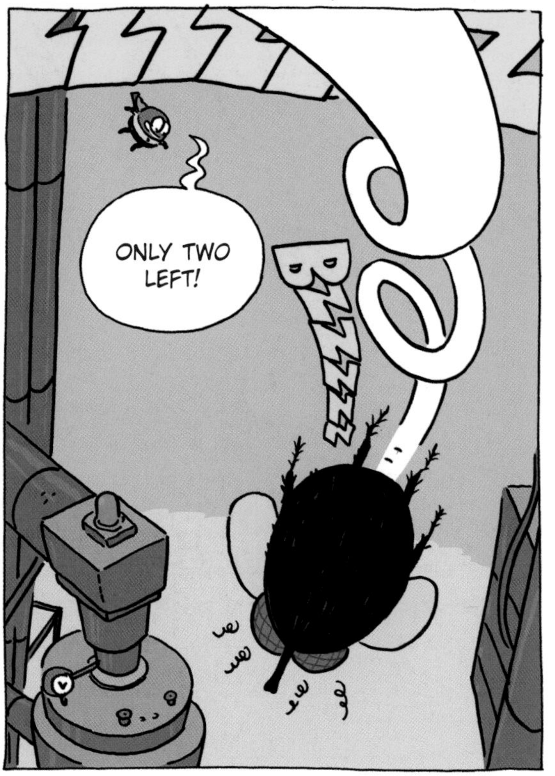
ONLY TWO LEFT!

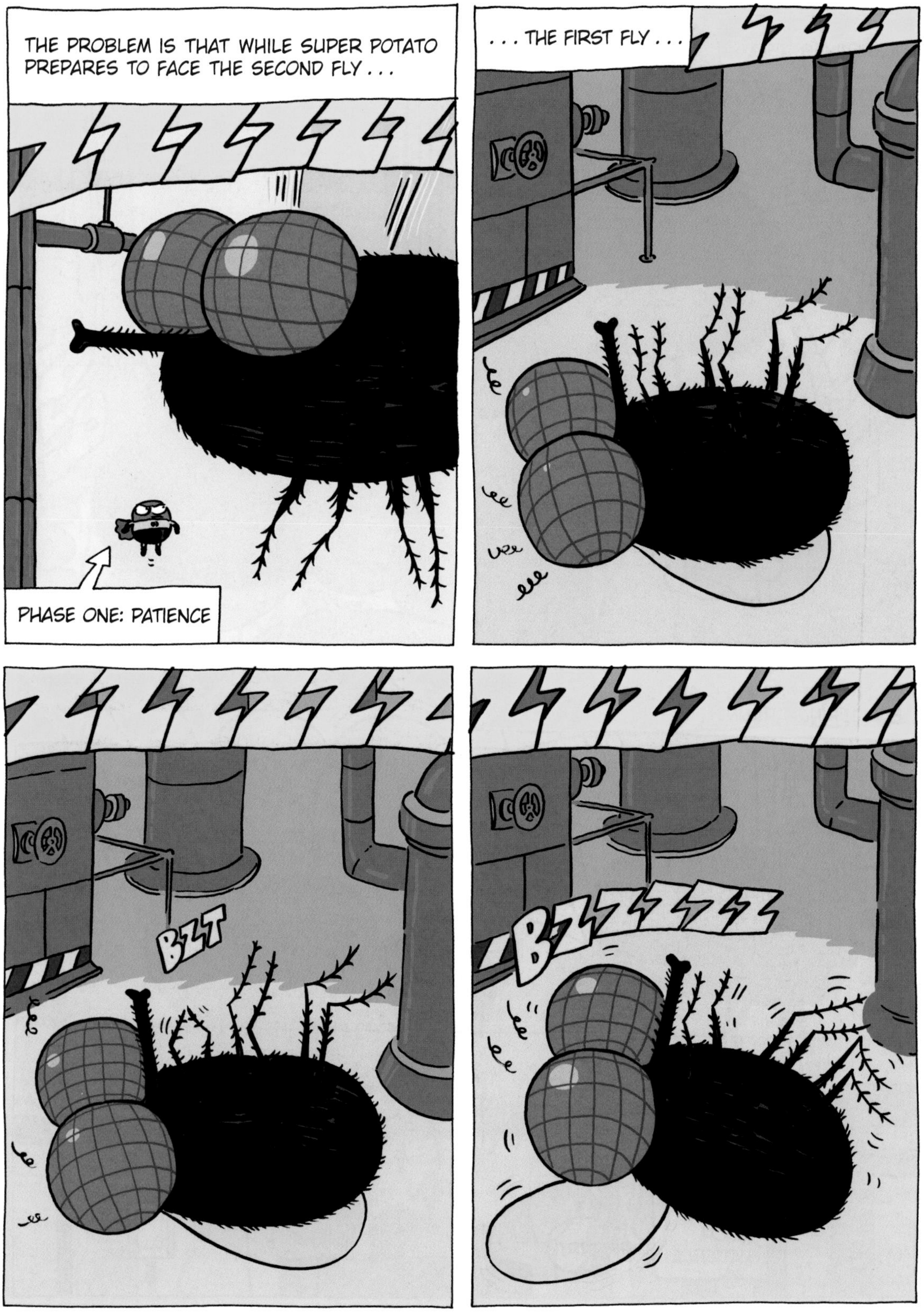
THE PROBLEM IS THAT WHILE SUPER POTATO PREPARES TO FACE THE SECOND FLY . . .
PHASE ONE: PATIENCE
. . . THE FIRST FLY . . .
BZT
BZZZZZZZ

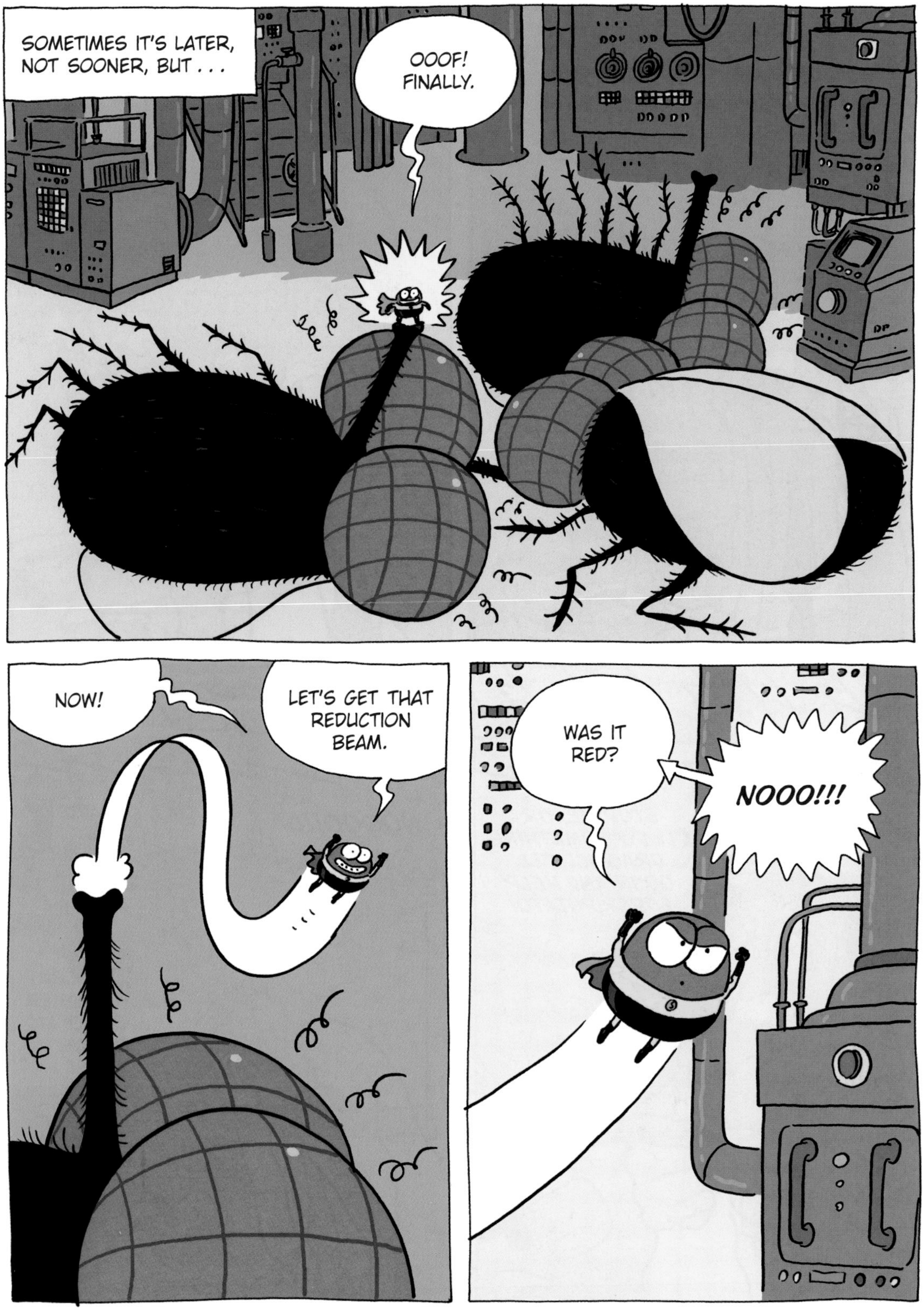
SOMETIMES IT'S LATER, NOT SOONER, BUT . . .
OOOF! FINALLY.
NOW!
LET'S GET THAT REDUCTION BEAM.
WAS IT RED?
NOOO!!!

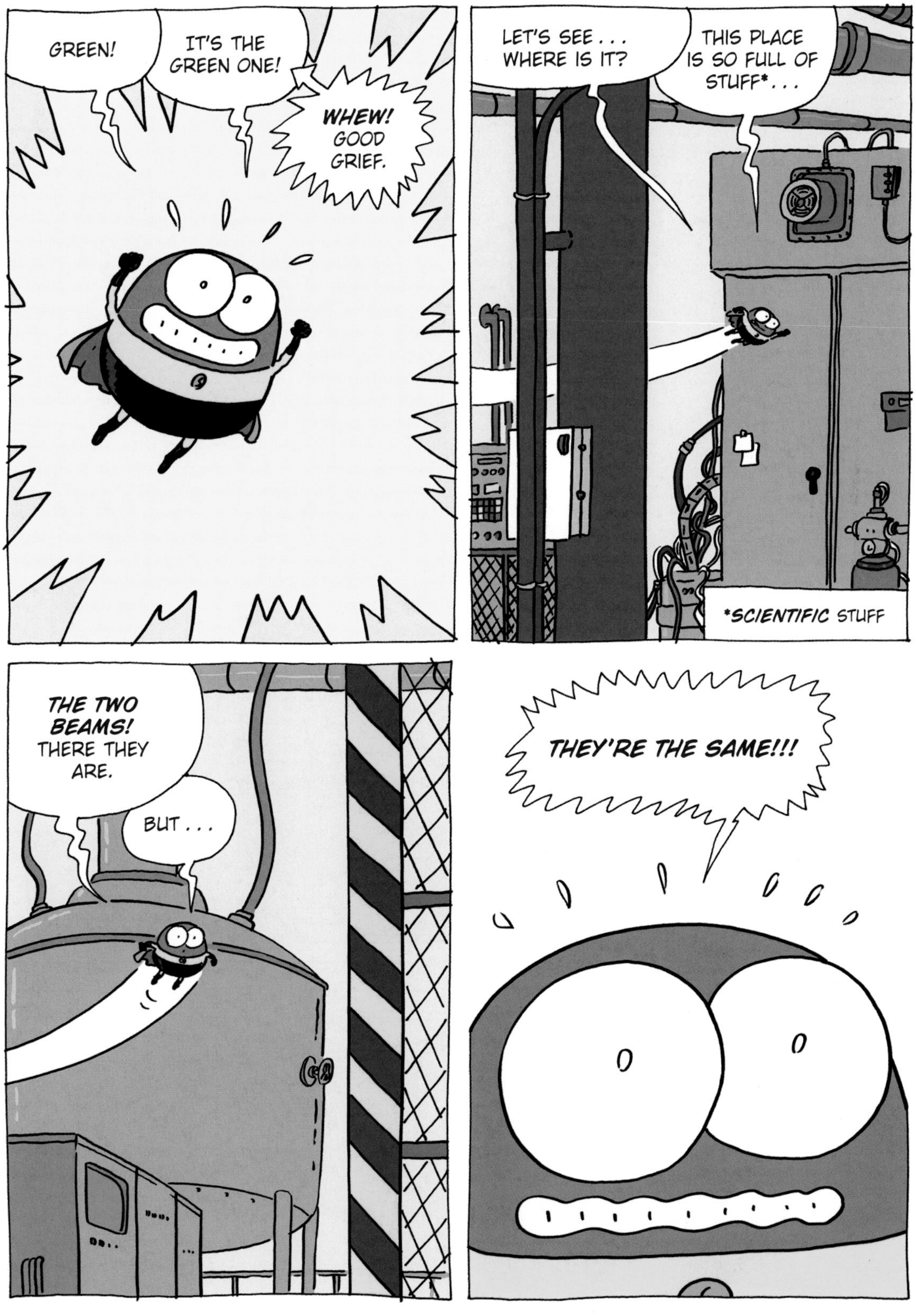
GREEN!
IT'S THE GREEN ONE!
WHEW! GOOD GRIEF.
LET'S SEE . . . WHERE IS IT?
THIS PLACE IS SO FULL OF STUFF* . . .
*SCIENTIFIC STUFF
THE TWO BEAMS! THERE THEY ARE.
BUT . . .
THEY'RE THE SAME!!!

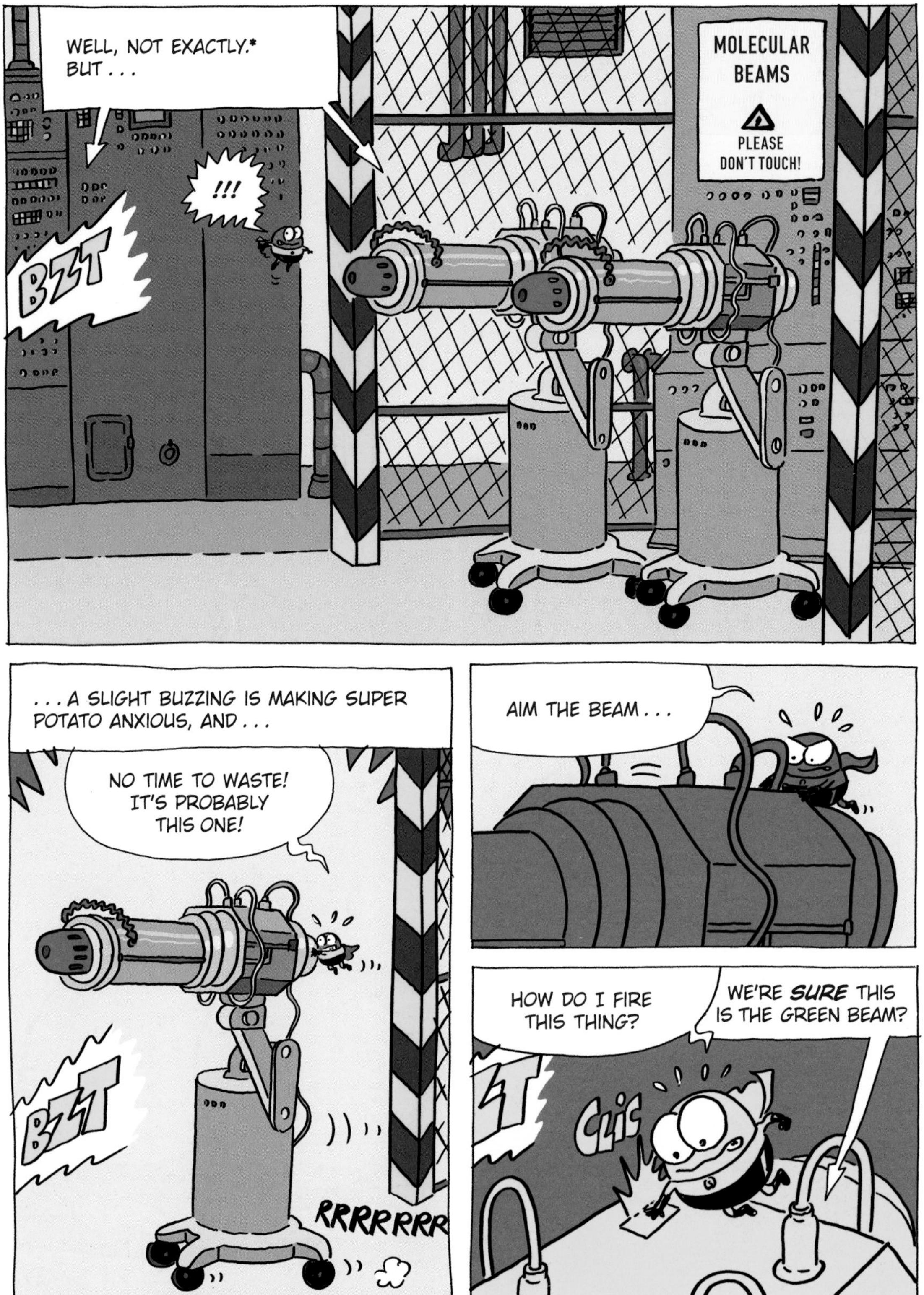
WELL, NOT EXACTLY.* BUT . . .
!!!
BZT
MOLECULAR BEAMS
PLEASE DON'T TOUCH!
. . . A SLIGHT BUZZING IS MAKING SUPER POTATO ANXIOUS, AND . . .
NO TIME TO WASTE! IT'S PROBABLY THIS ONE!
BZT
RRRRRRR
AIM THE BEAM . . .
HOW DO I FIRE THIS THING?
WE'RE ***SURE*** THIS IS THE GREEN BEAM?
CLIC

*TO RECALL THE MINOR DIFFERENCES, FLIP BACK TO PAGE 7

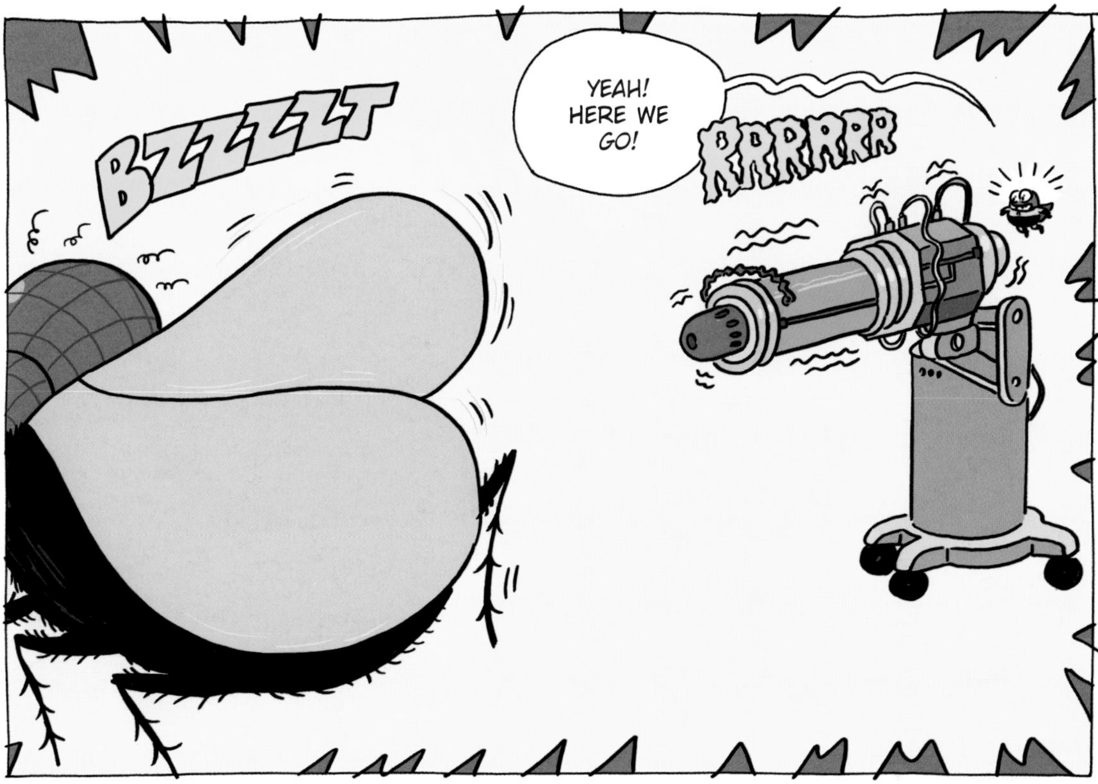
BZZZZLT
YEAH! HERE WE GO!
RRRRRR

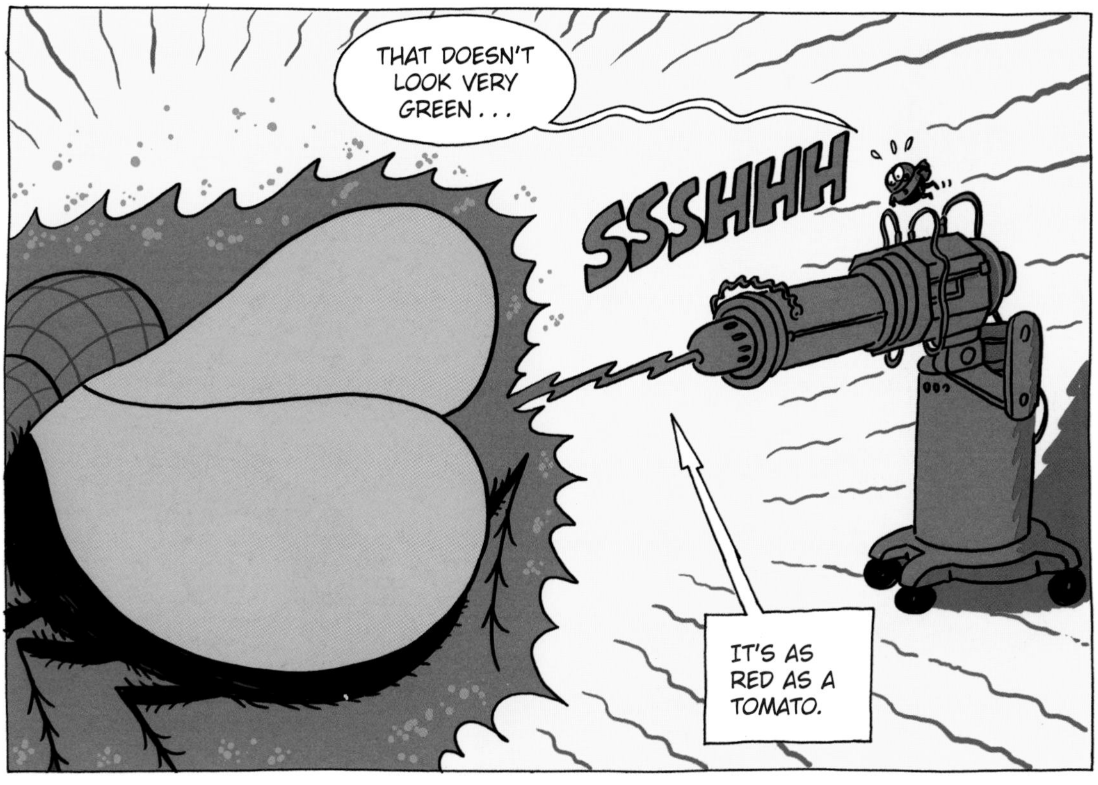
THAT DOESN'T LOOK VERY GREEN . . .
SSSHHH
IT'S AS RED AS A TOMATO.

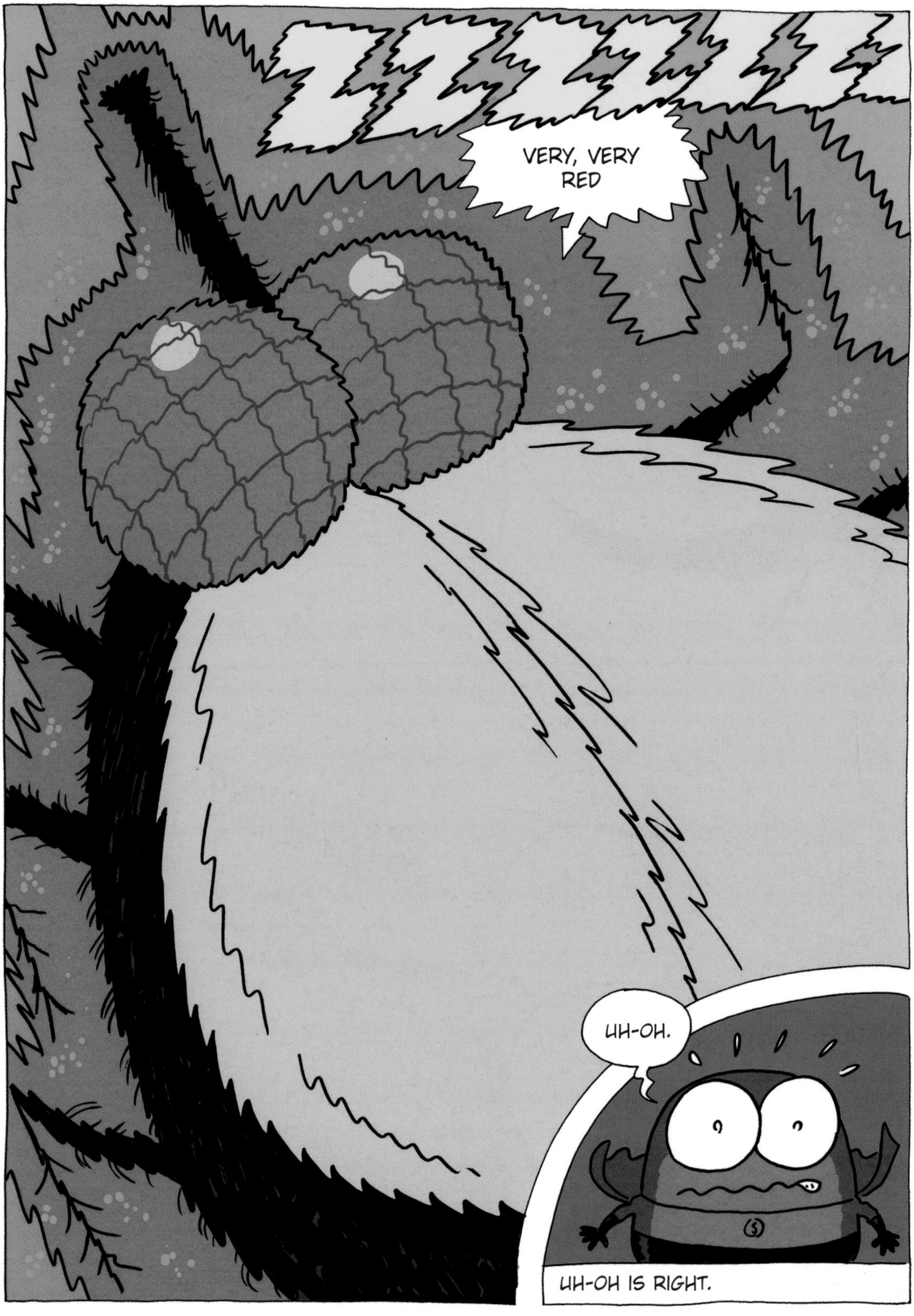
ZZZZZZ
VERY, VERY RED
UH-OH.
UH-OH IS RIGHT.

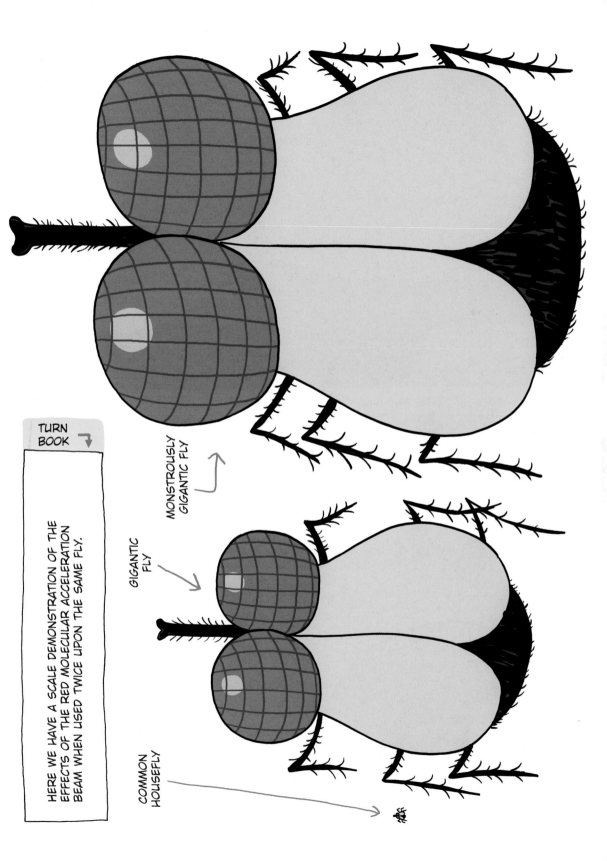

TURN BOOK →

HERE WE HAVE A SCALE DEMONSTRATION OF THE EFFECTS OF THE RED MOLECULAR ACCELERATION BEAM WHEN USED TWICE UPON THE SAME FLY.

MONSTROUSLY GIGANTIC FLY

GIGANTIC FLY

COMMON HOUSEFLY

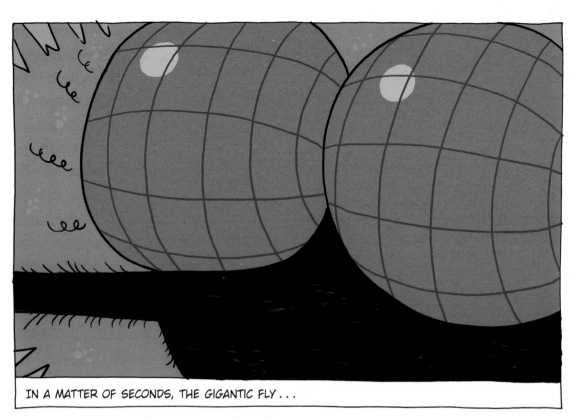

IN A MATTER OF SECONDS, THE GIGANTIC FLY . . .

. . . HAS BECOME A MONSTROUS ONE, AND IT'S READY TO TAKE FLIGHT.

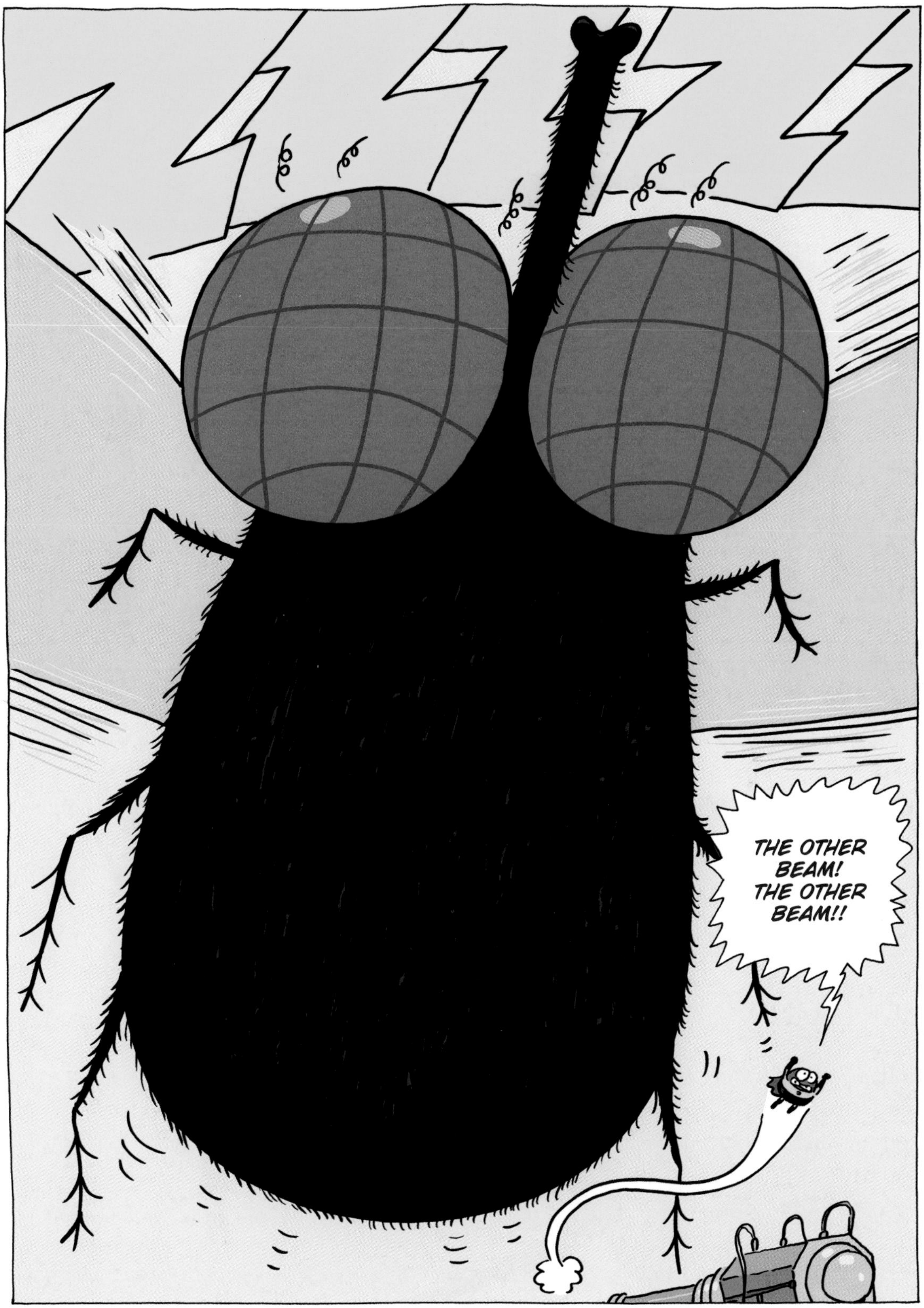
THE OTHER BEAM! THE OTHER BEAM!!

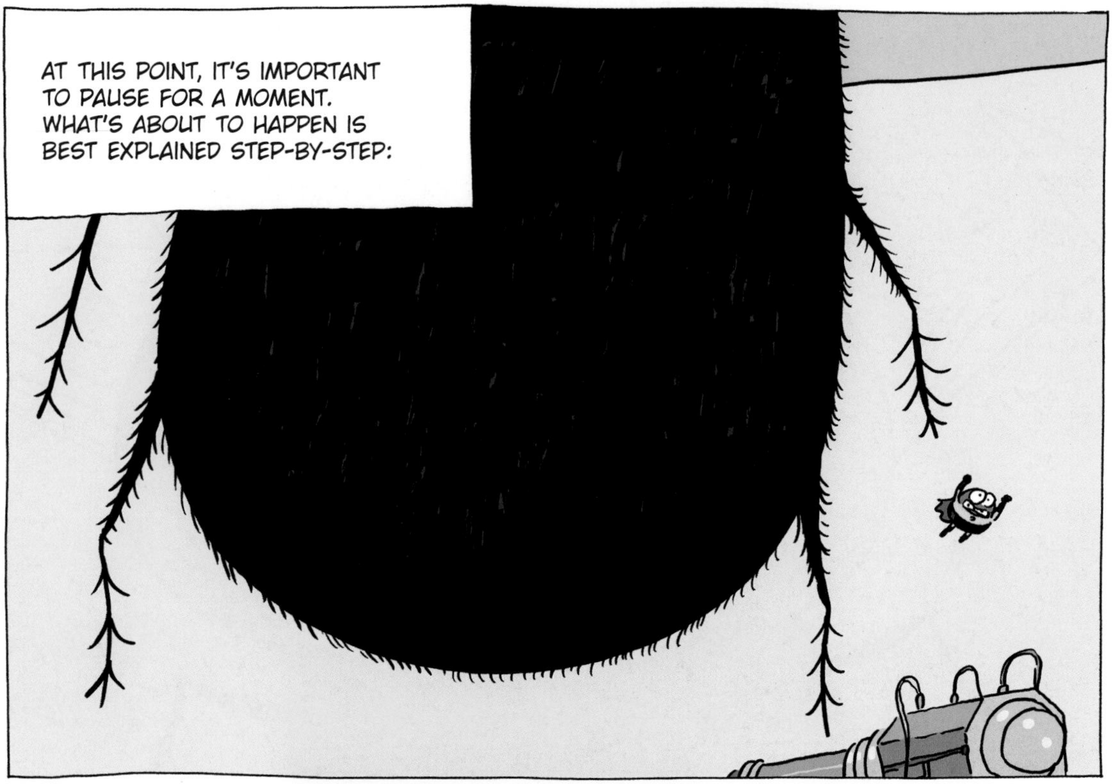
AT THIS POINT, IT'S IMPORTANT TO PAUSE FOR A MOMENT. WHAT'S ABOUT TO HAPPEN IS BEST EXPLAINED STEP-BY-STEP:
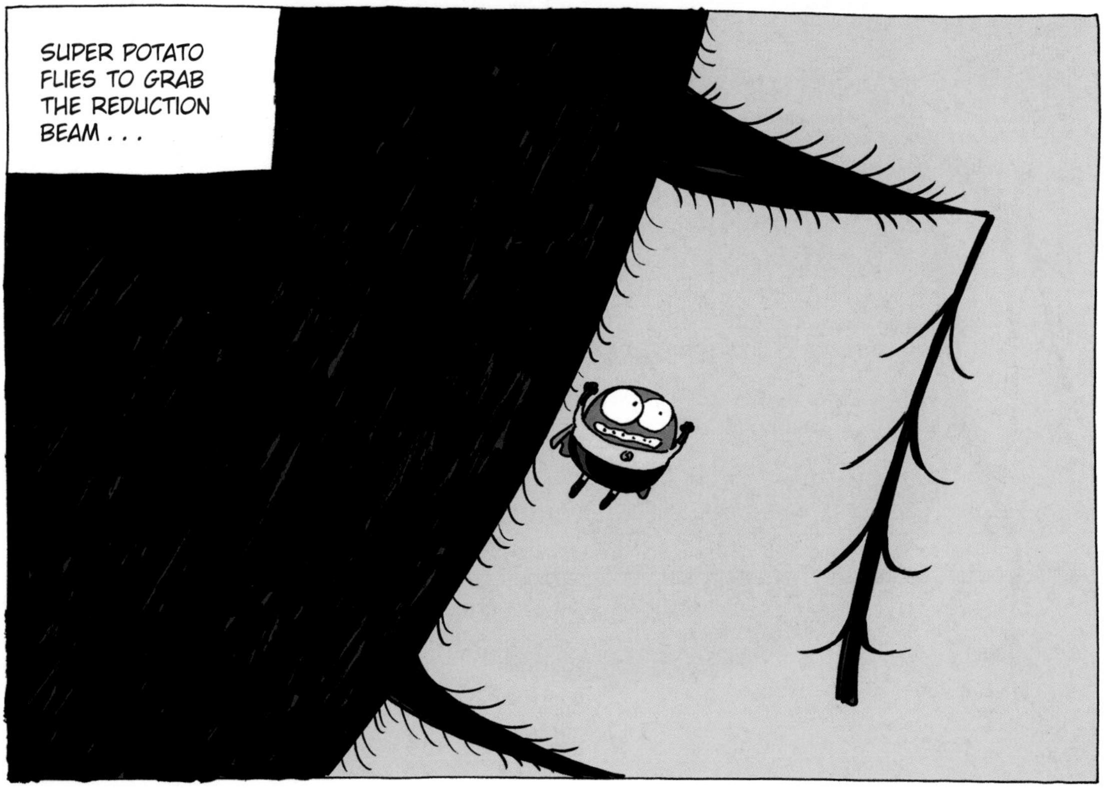
SUPER POTATO FLIES TO GRAB THE REDUCTION BEAM . . .

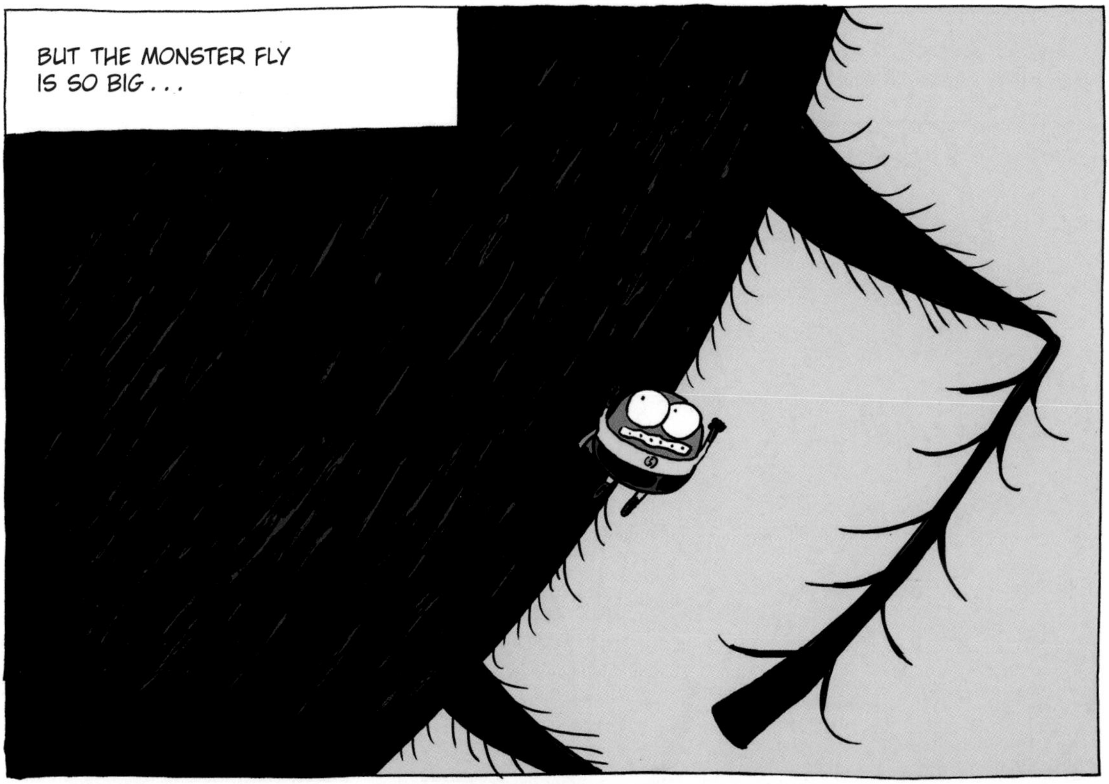
BUT THE MONSTER FLY IS SO BIG . . .

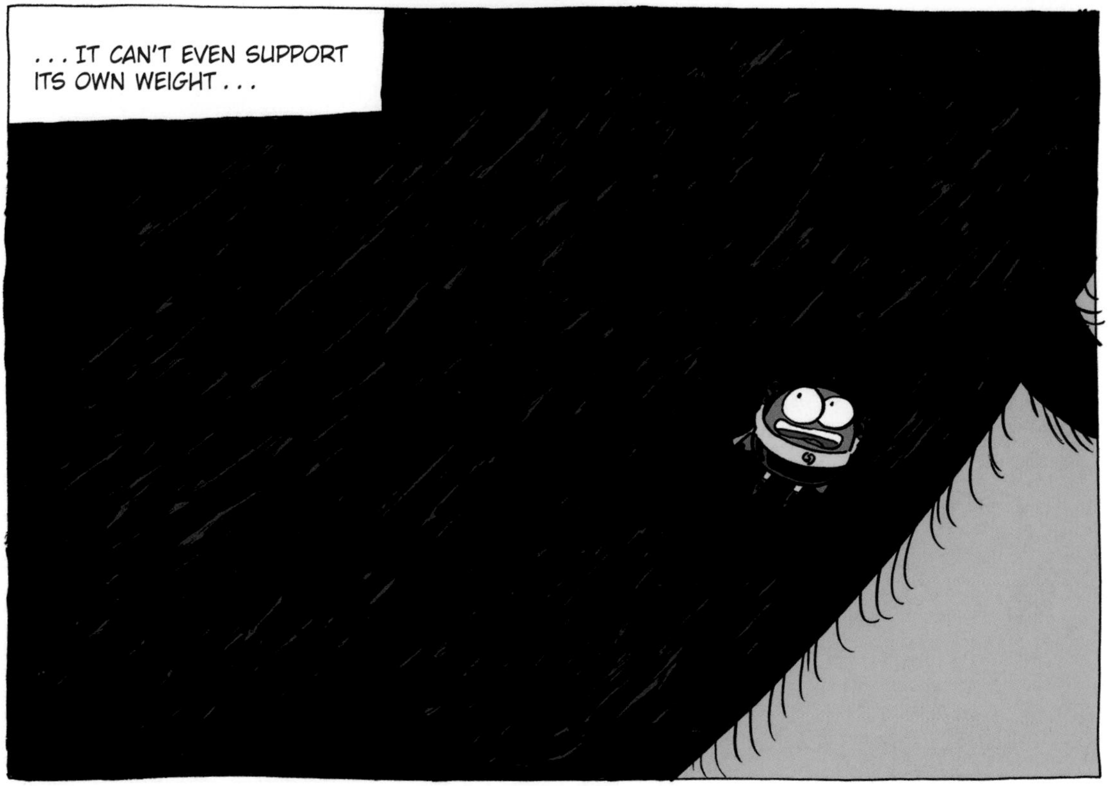
. . . IT CAN'T EVEN SUPPORT ITS OWN WEIGHT . . .

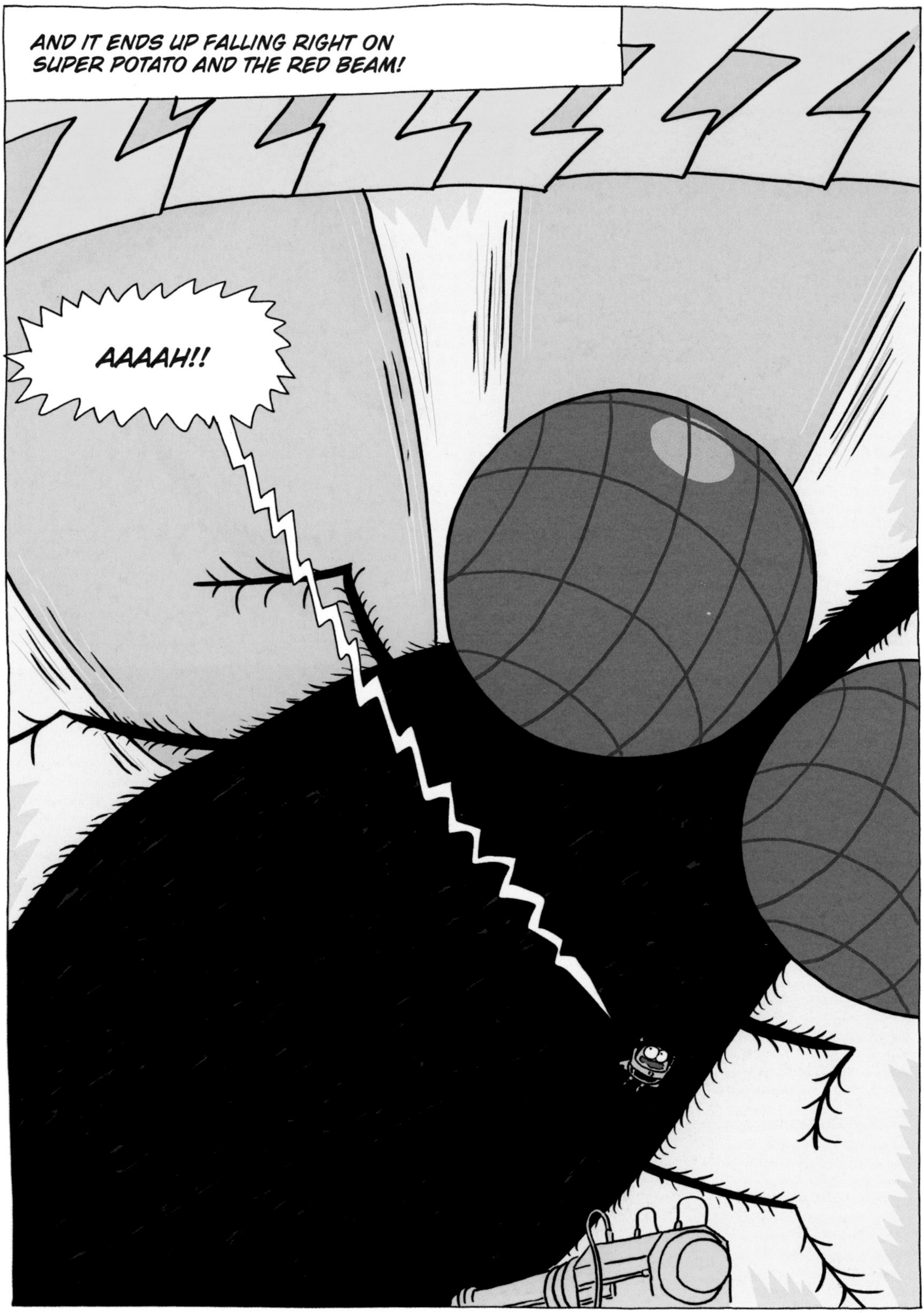
AND IT ENDS UP FALLING RIGHT ON SUPER POTATO AND THE RED BEAM!
AAAAH!!

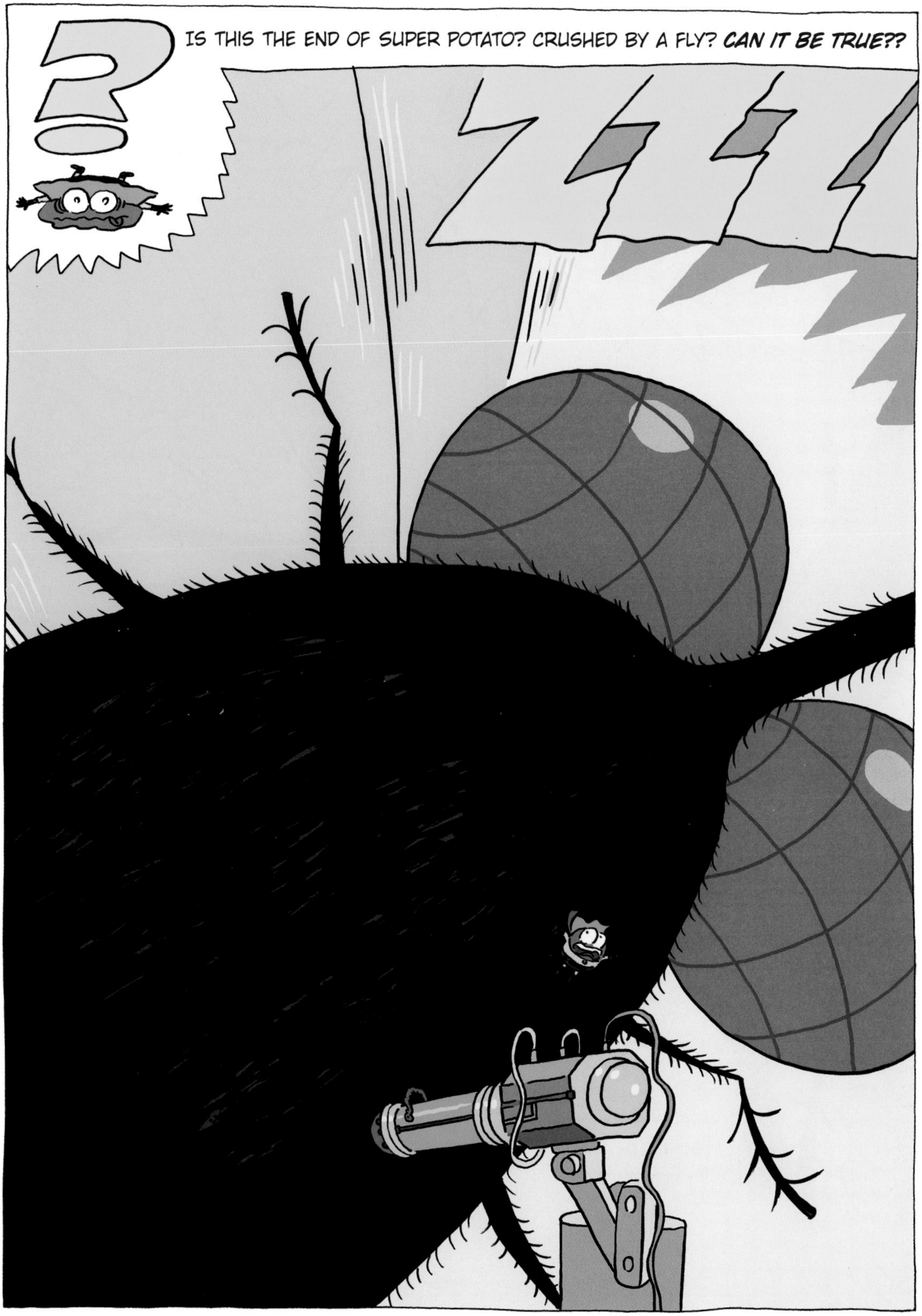
IS THIS THE END OF SUPER POTATO? CRUSHED BY A FLY? CAN IT BE TRUE??

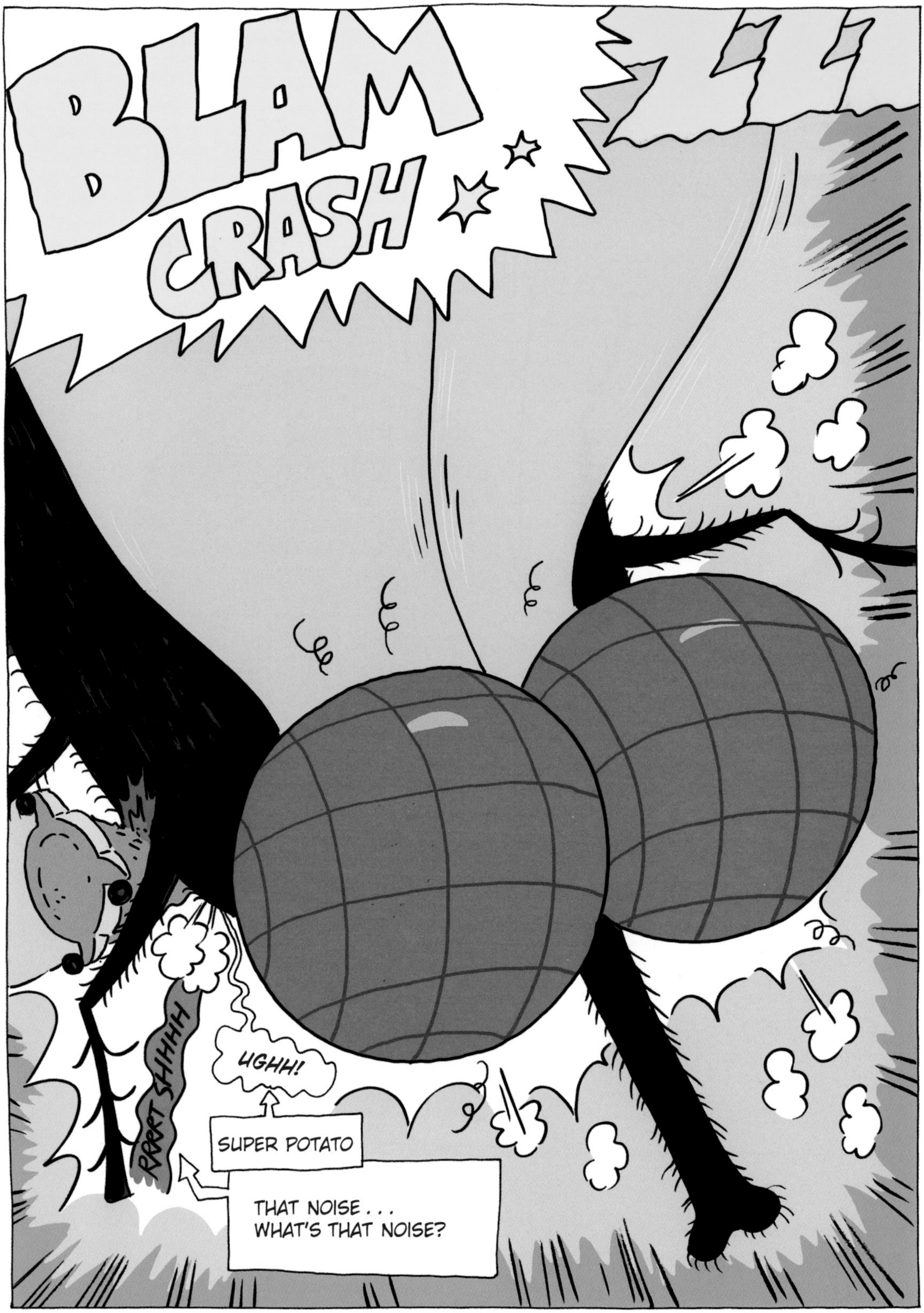
BLAM
CRASH
ZZZ
RRRRT SHHHH
UGHH!
SUPER POTATO
THAT NOISE . . .
WHAT'S THAT NOISE?

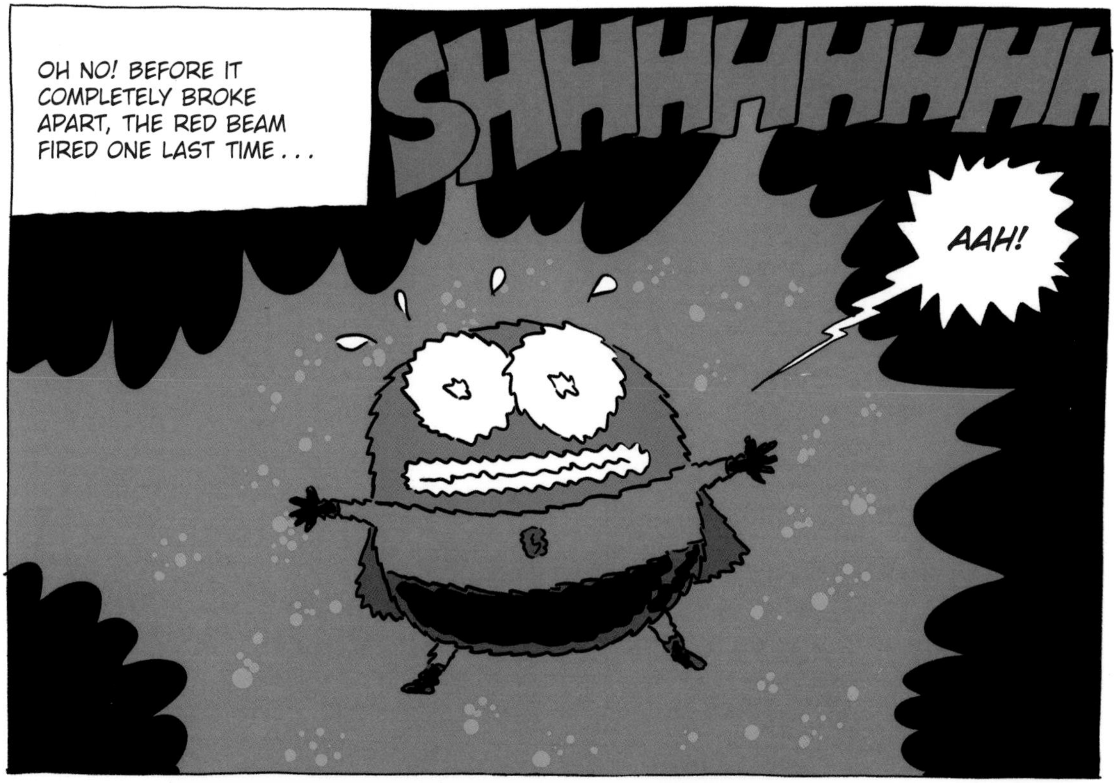
OH NO! BEFORE IT COMPLETELY BROKE APART, THE RED BEAM FIRED ONE LAST TIME . . .
SHHHHHHHH
AAH!

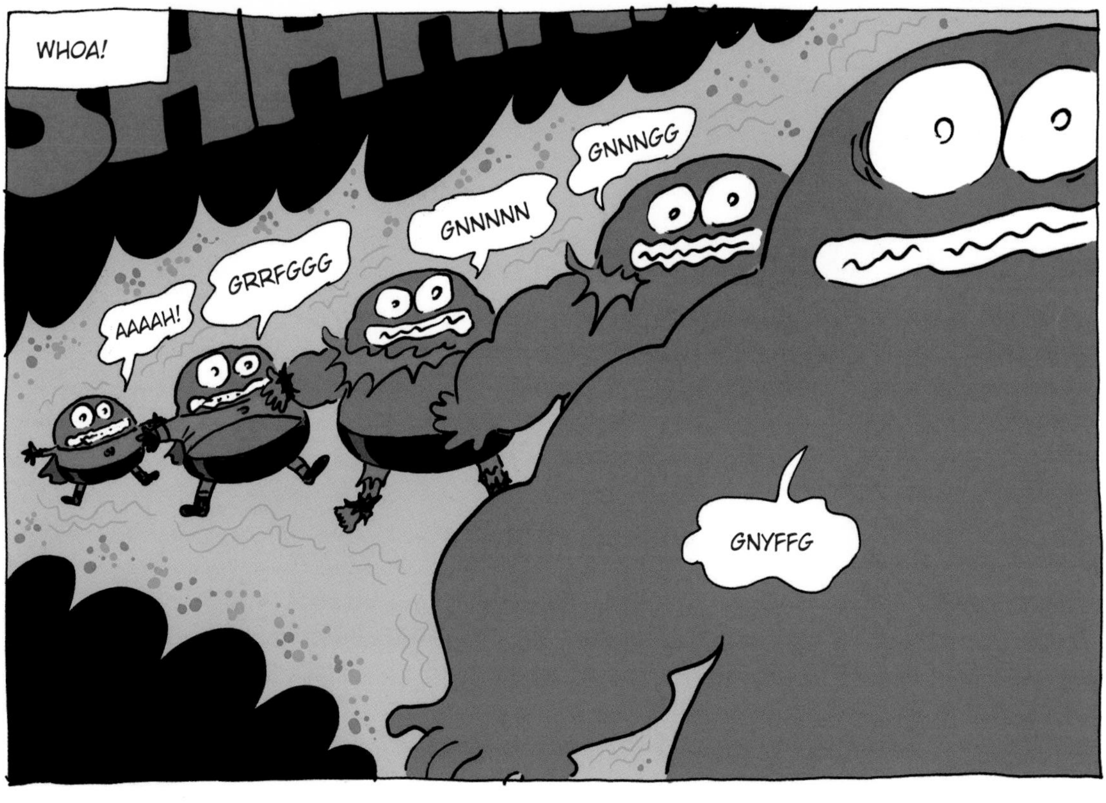
WHOA!
GNNNGG
GNNNNN
GRRFGGG
AAAAH!
GNYFFG

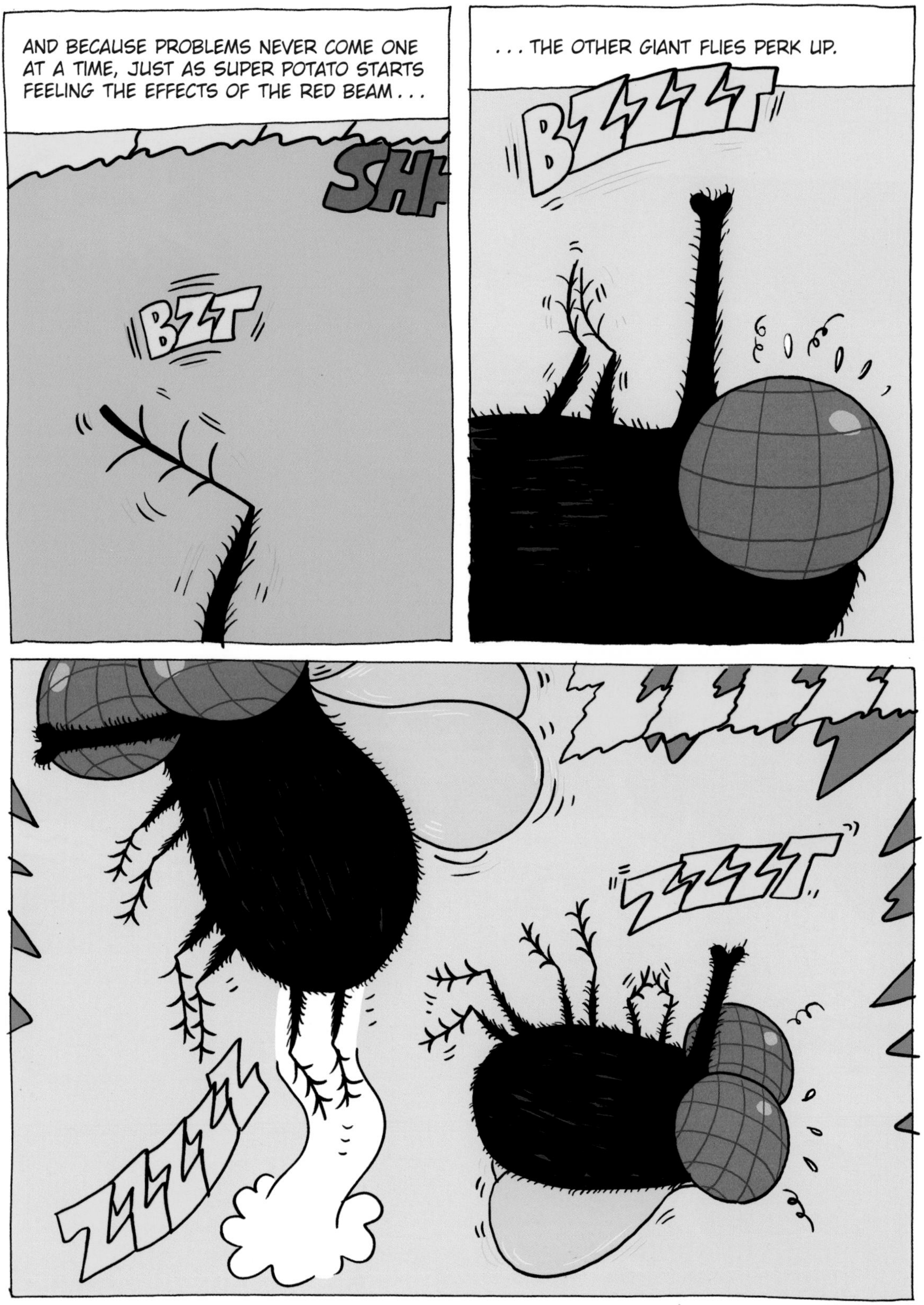
AND BECAUSE PROBLEMS NEVER COME ONE AT A TIME, JUST AS SUPER POTATO STARTS FEELING THE EFFECTS OF THE RED BEAM . . .
SH
BZT
. . . THE OTHER GIANT FLIES PERK UP.
BZZZZT
ZZZZZ
ZZZZT

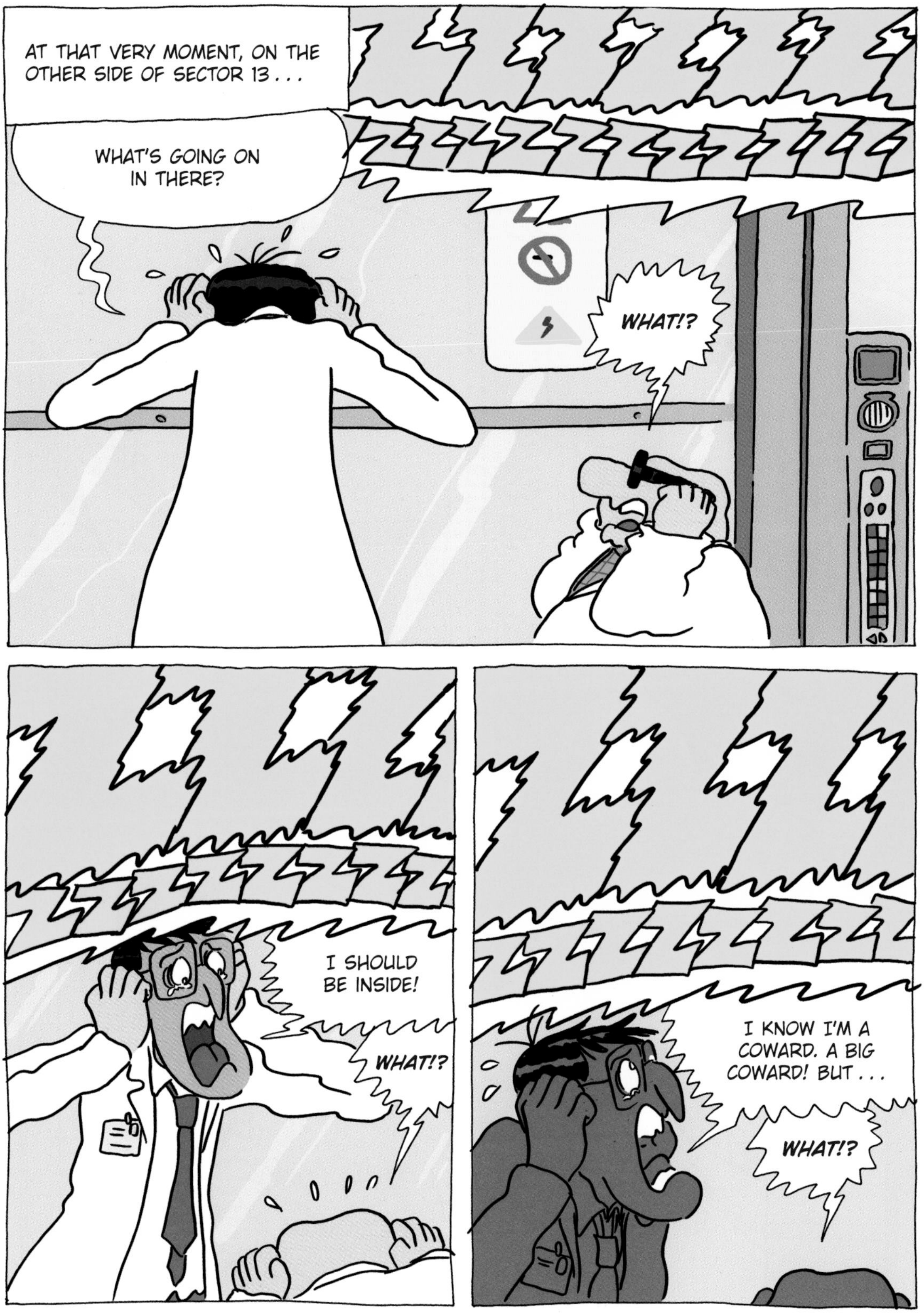

AT THAT VERY MOMENT, ON THE OTHER SIDE OF SECTOR 13 . . .
WHAT'S GOING ON IN THERE?
WHAT!?
I SHOULD BE INSIDE!
WHAT!?
I KNOW I'M A COWARD. A BIG COWARD! BUT . . .
WHAT!?

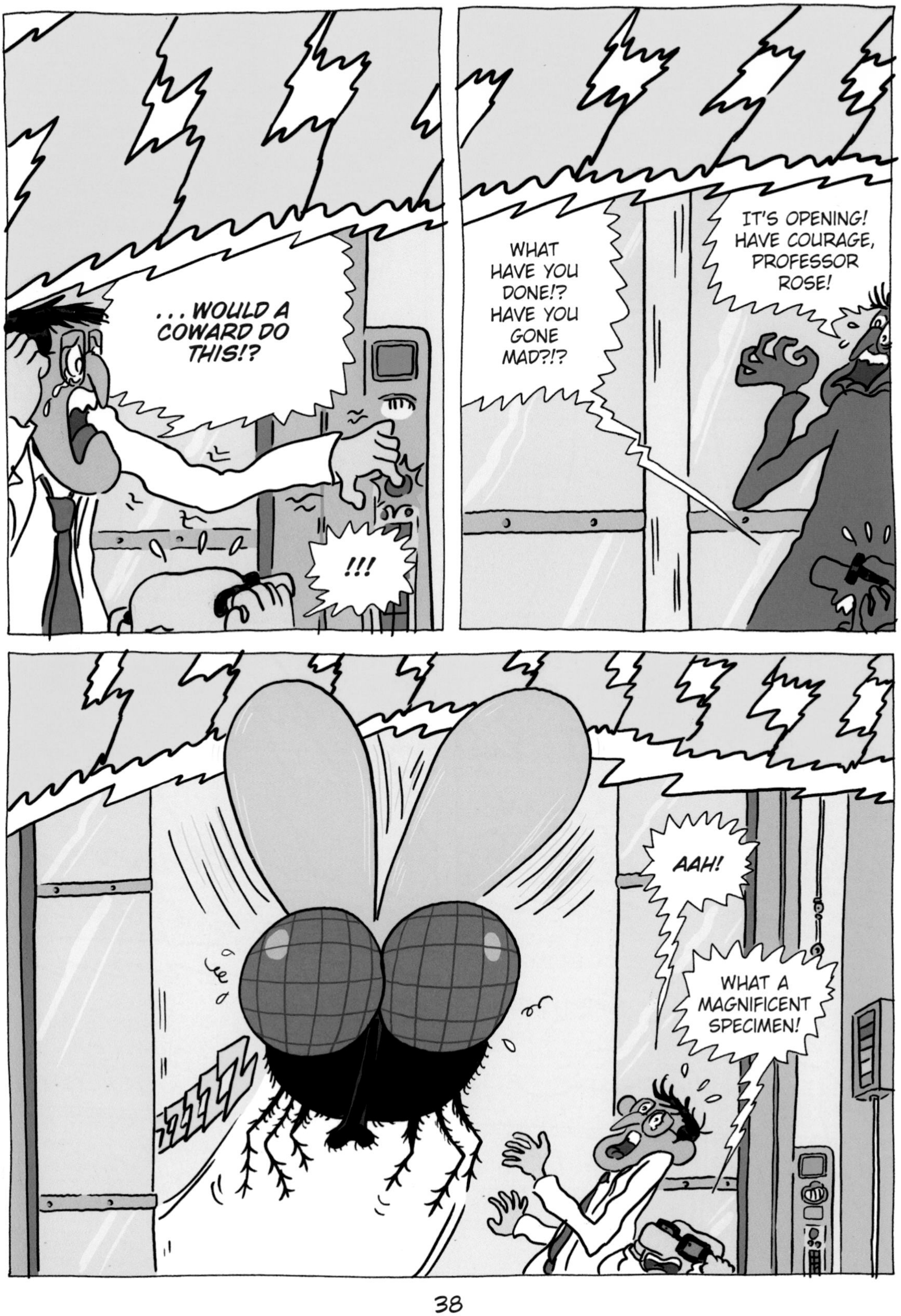
...WOULD A COWARD DO THIS!?
!!!
WHAT HAVE YOU DONE!? HAVE YOU GONE MAD?!?
IT'S OPENING! HAVE COURAGE, PROFESSOR ROSE!
AAH!
WHAT A MAGNIFICENT SPECIMEN!
ZZZZZ

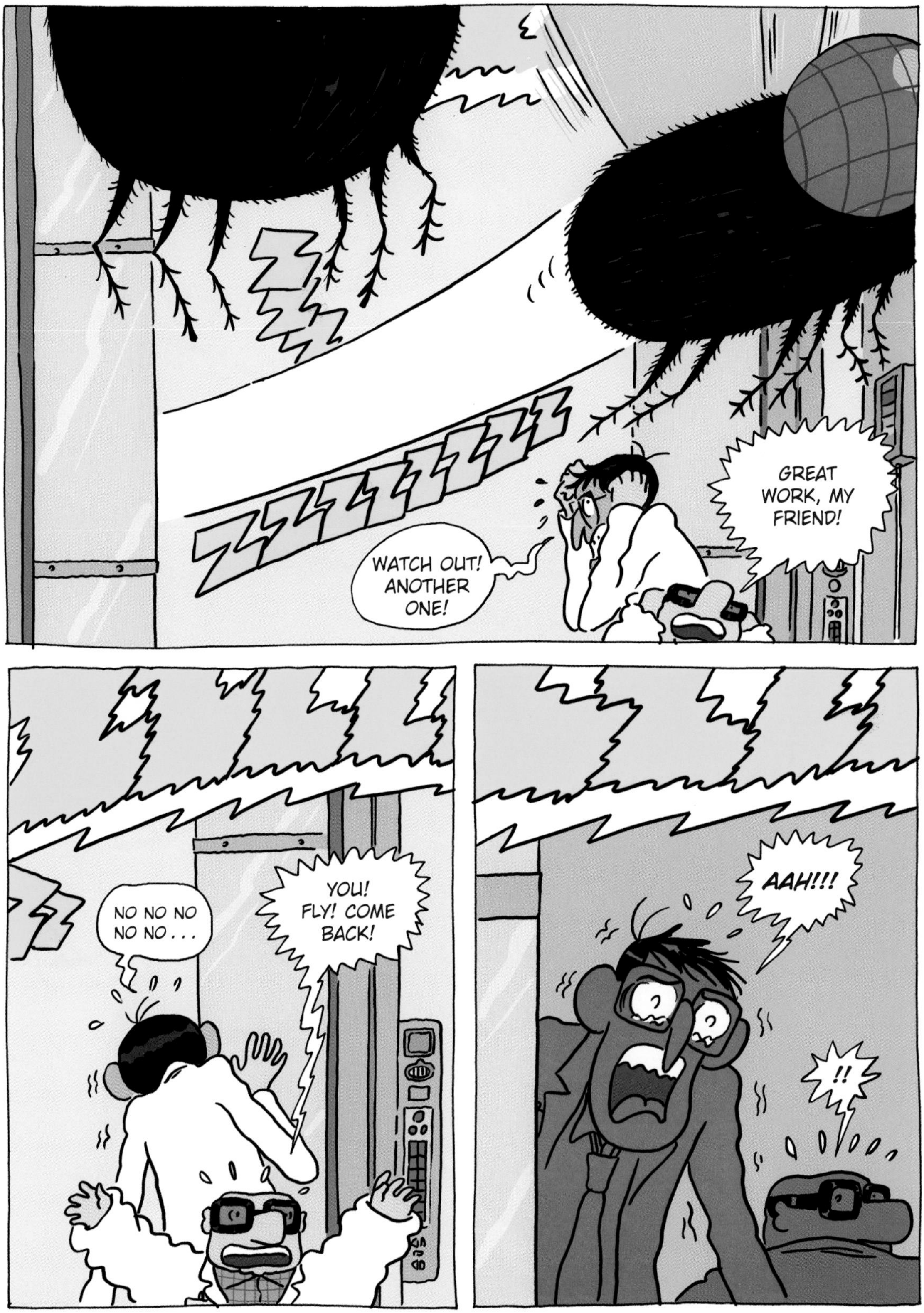
ZZZZZZZZZ
GREAT WORK, MY FRIEND!
WATCH OUT! ANOTHER ONE!
NO NO NO NO NO . . .
YOU! FLY! COME BACK!
AAH!!!
!!

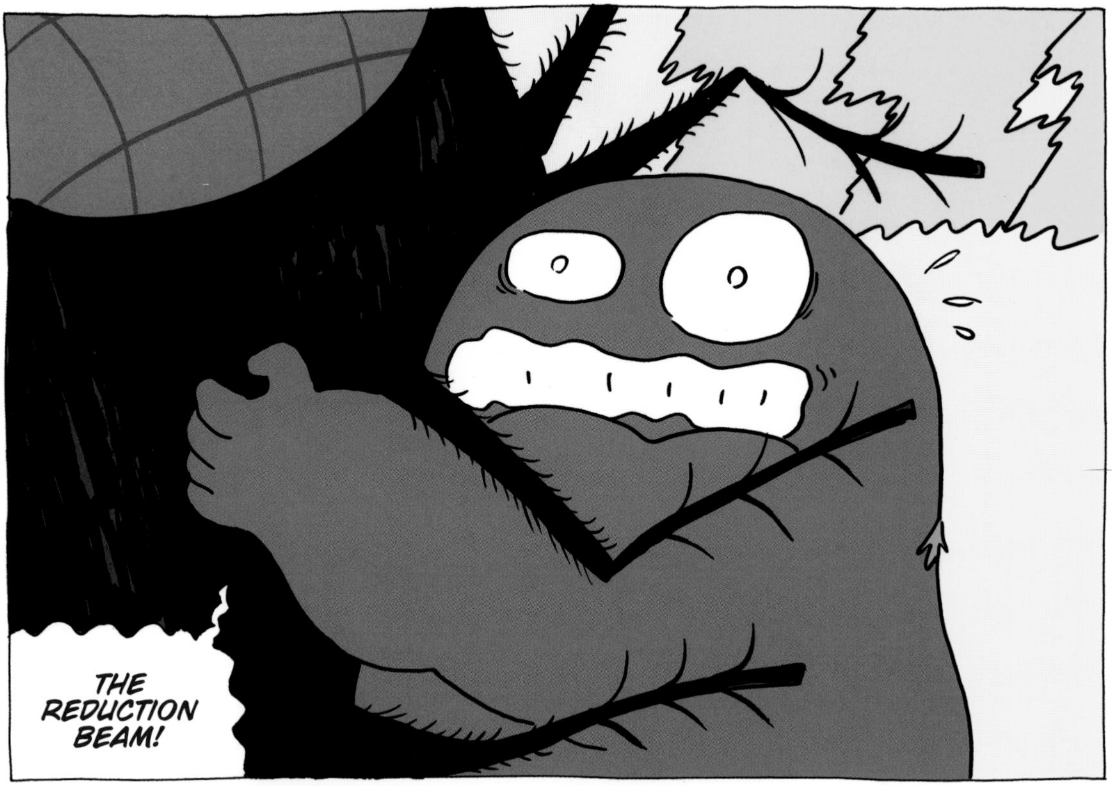
THE REDUCTION BEAM!

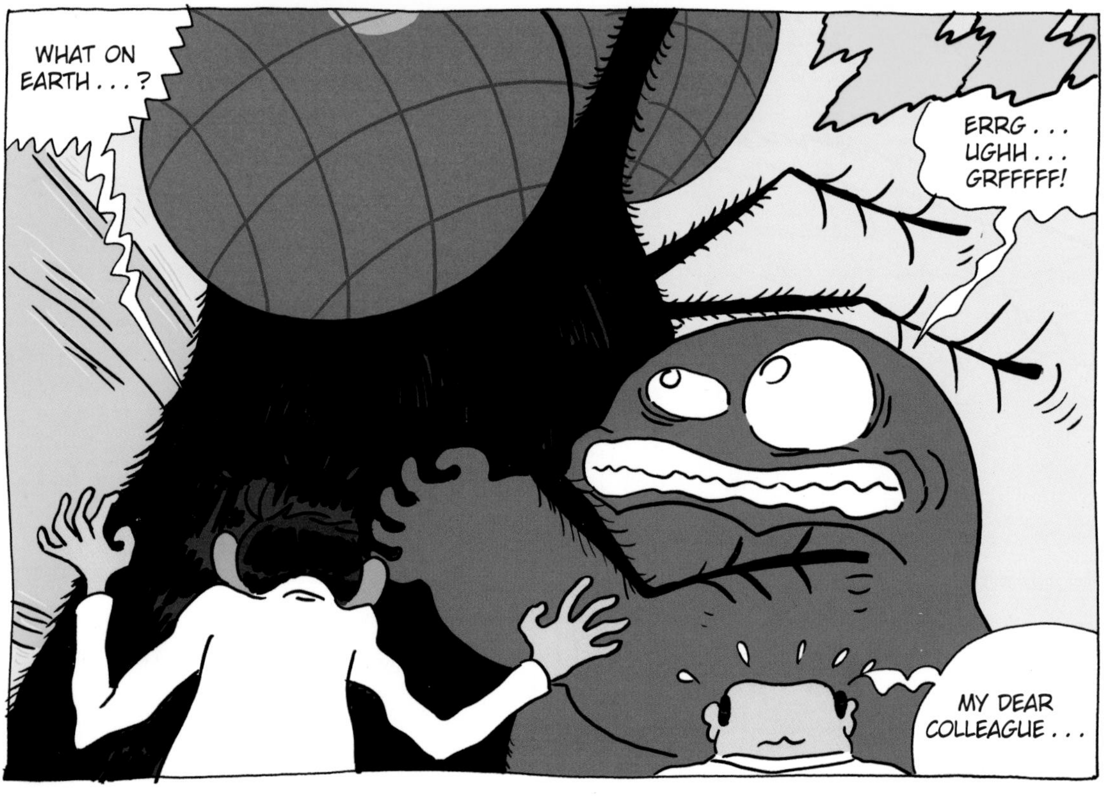
WHAT ON EARTH . . . ?
ERRG . . . UGHH . . . GRFFFFF!
MY DEAR COLLEAGUE . . .

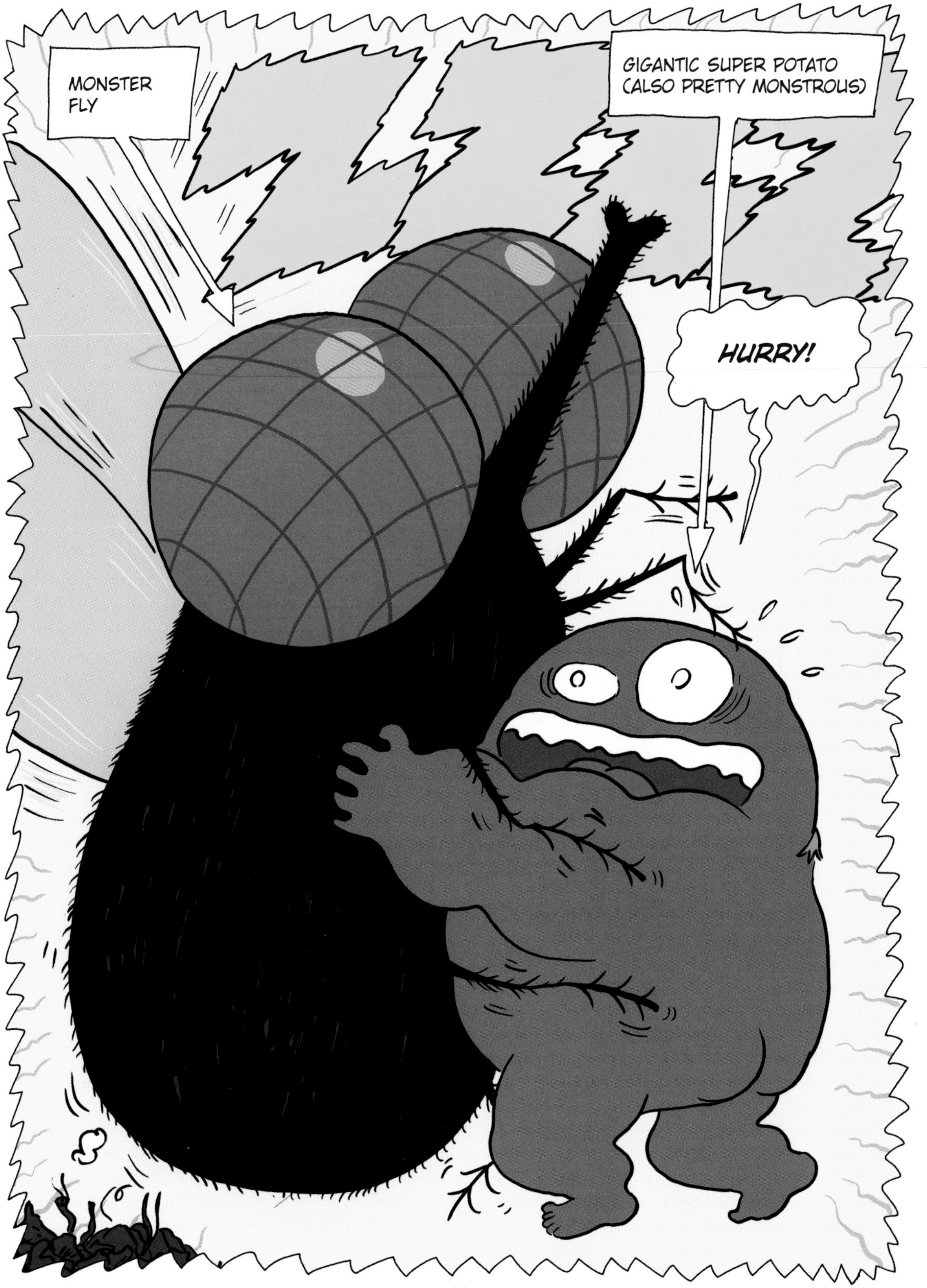
MONSTER FLY
GIGANTIC SUPER POTATO (ALSO PRETTY MONSTROUS)
HURRY!

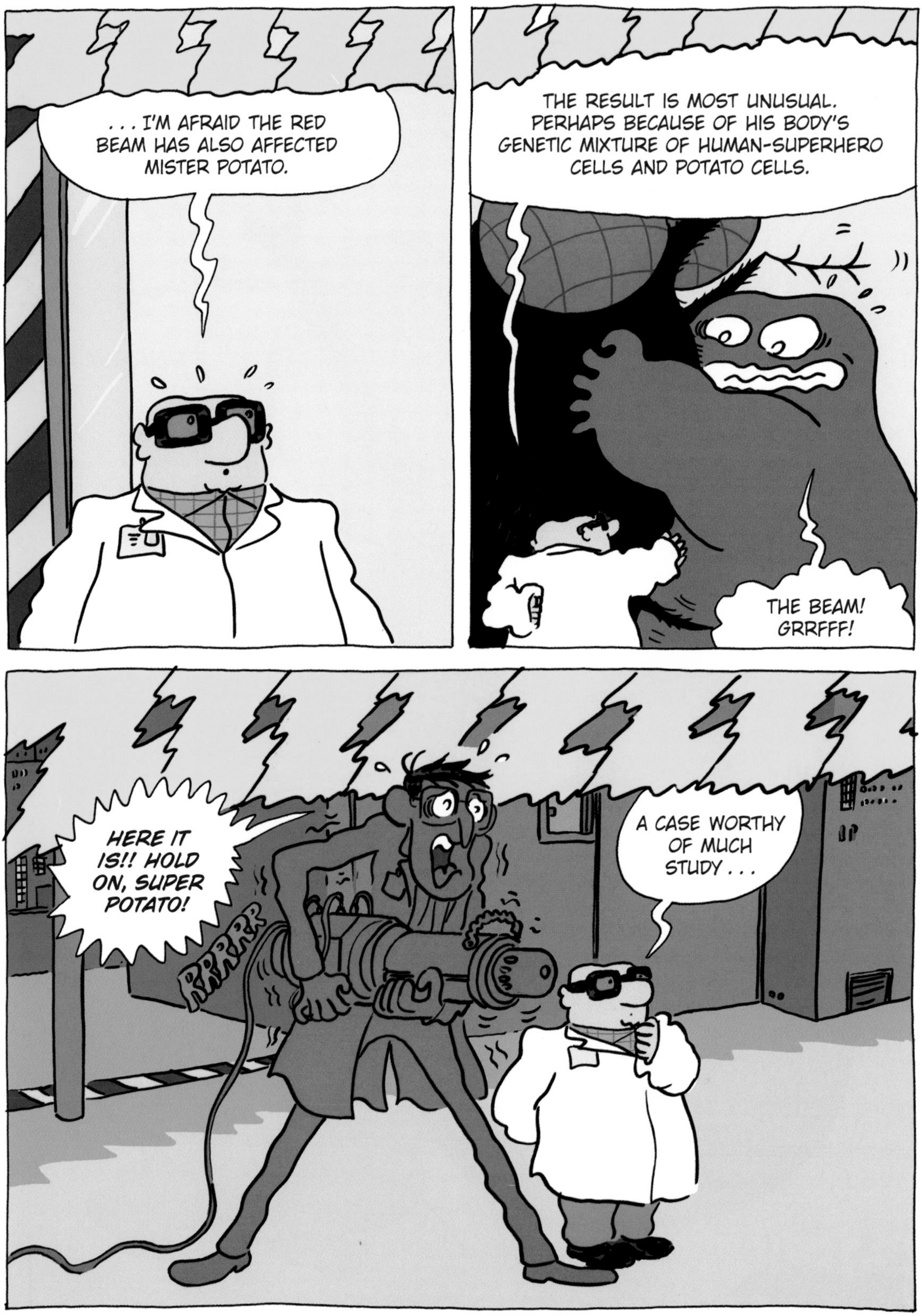
. . . I'M AFRAID THE RED BEAM HAS ALSO AFFECTED MISTER POTATO.
THE RESULT IS MOST UNUSUAL. PERHAPS BECAUSE OF HIS BODY'S GENETIC MIXTURE OF HUMAN-SUPERHERO CELLS AND POTATO CELLS.
THE BEAM! GRRFFF!
HERE IT IS!! HOLD ON, SUPER POTATO!
RRRRRR
A CASE WORTHY OF MUCH STUDY . . .

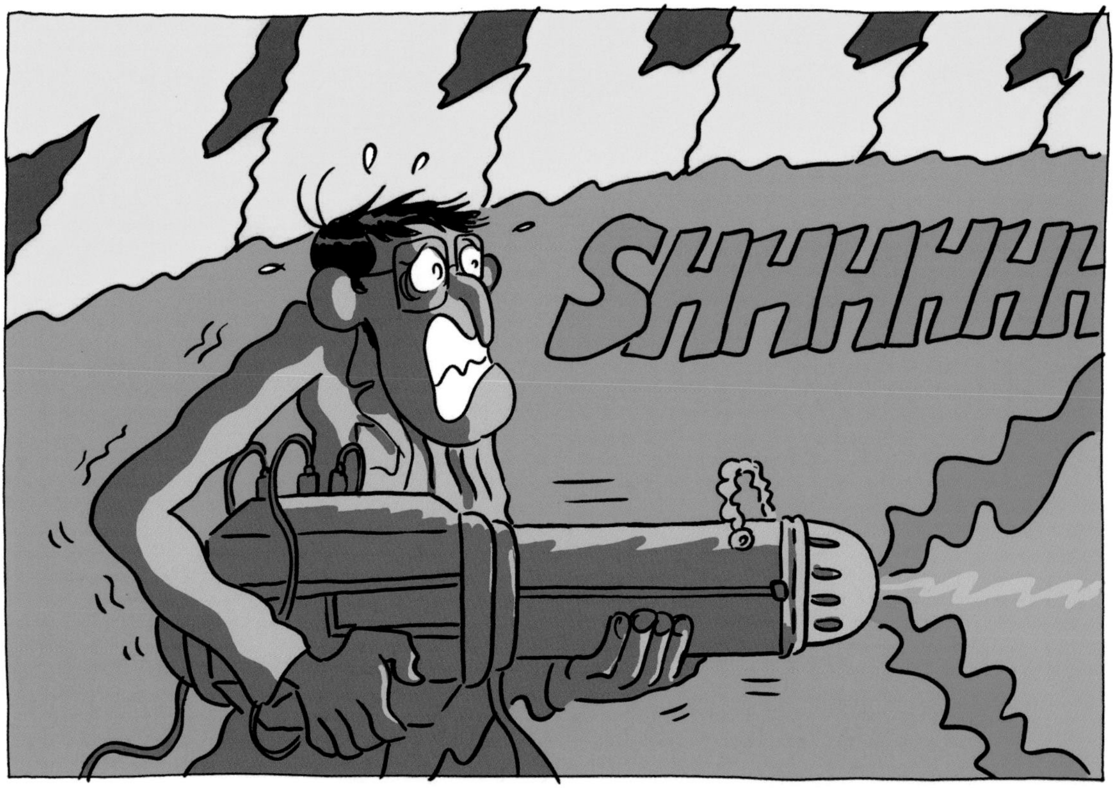
SHHHHH

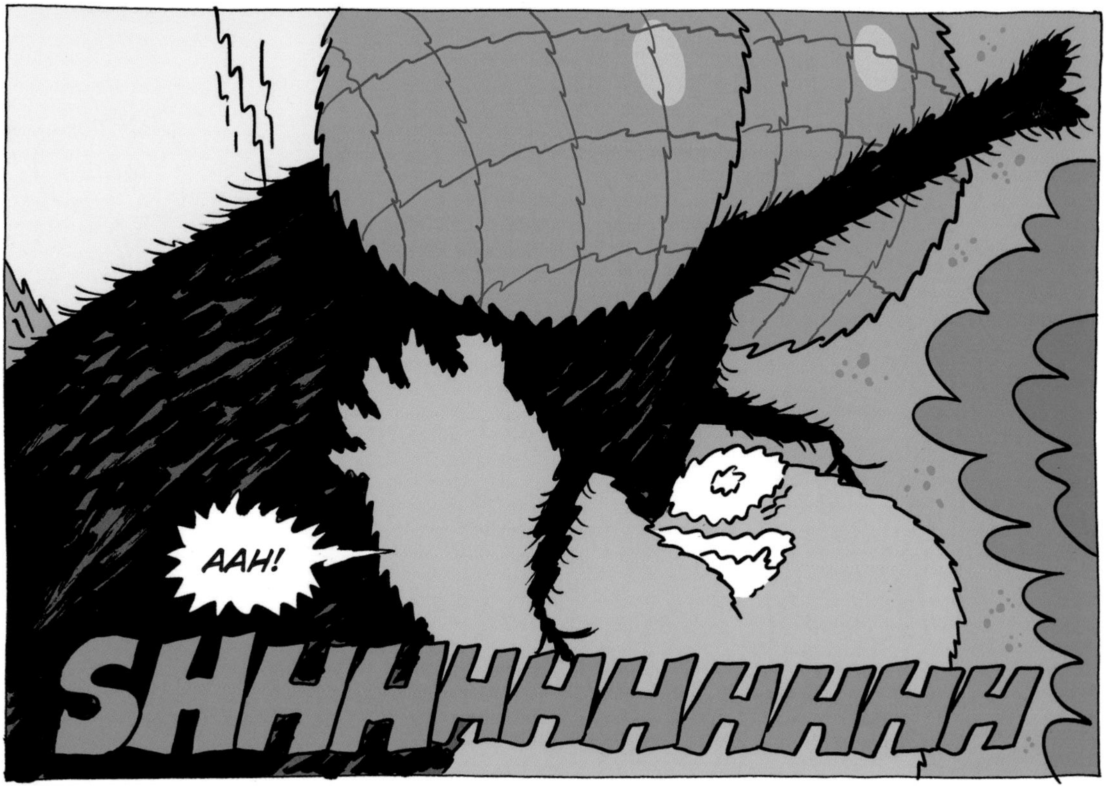
AAH!
SHHHHHHHHHHH

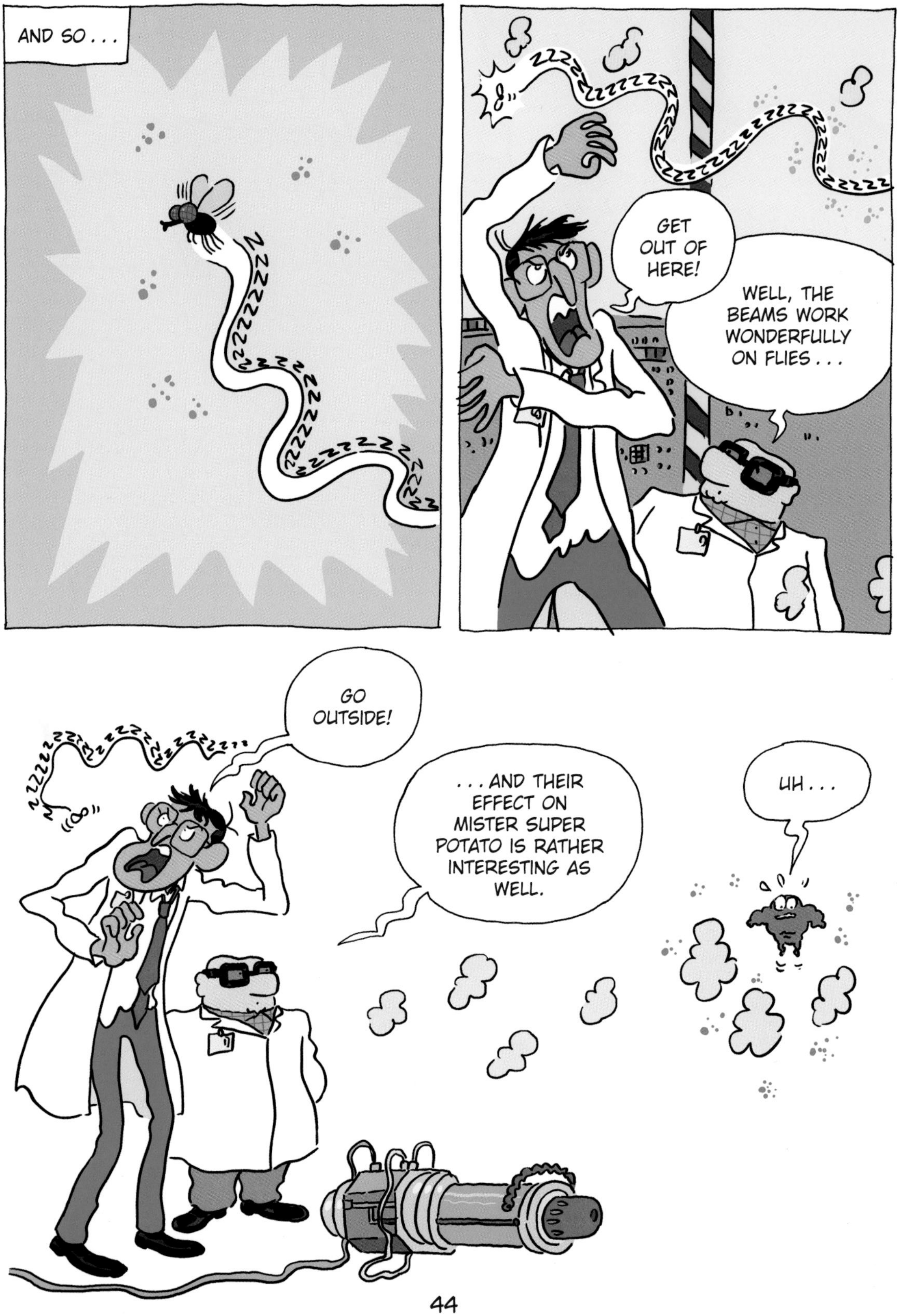
AND SO . . .
GET OUT OF HERE!
WELL, THE BEAMS WORK WONDERFULLY ON FLIES . . .
GO OUTSIDE!
. . . AND THEIR EFFECT ON MISTER SUPER POTATO IS RATHER INTERESTING AS WELL.
UH . . .

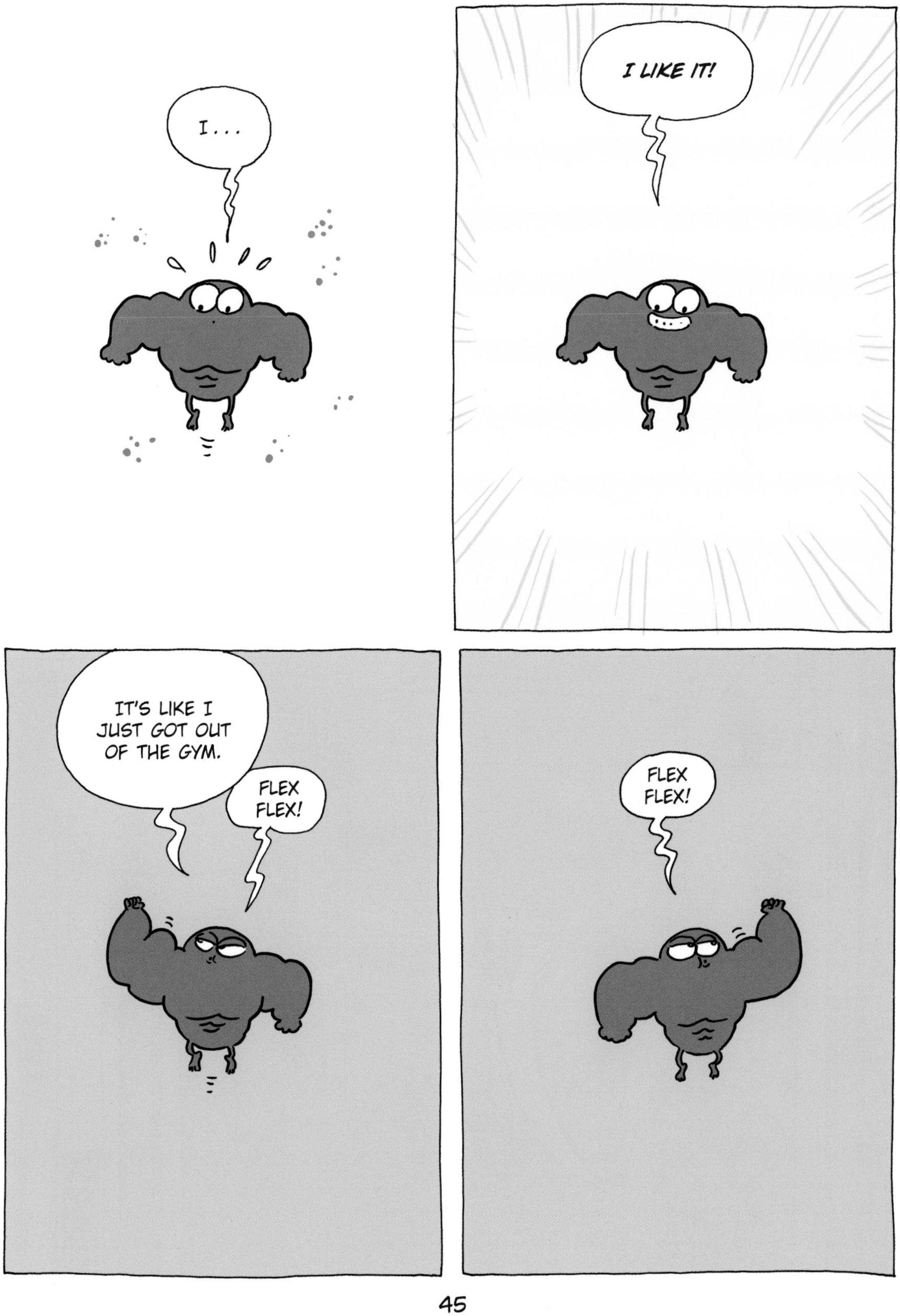
I . . .
I LIKE IT!
IT'S LIKE I JUST GOT OUT OF THE GYM.
FLEX FLEX!
FLEX FLEX!

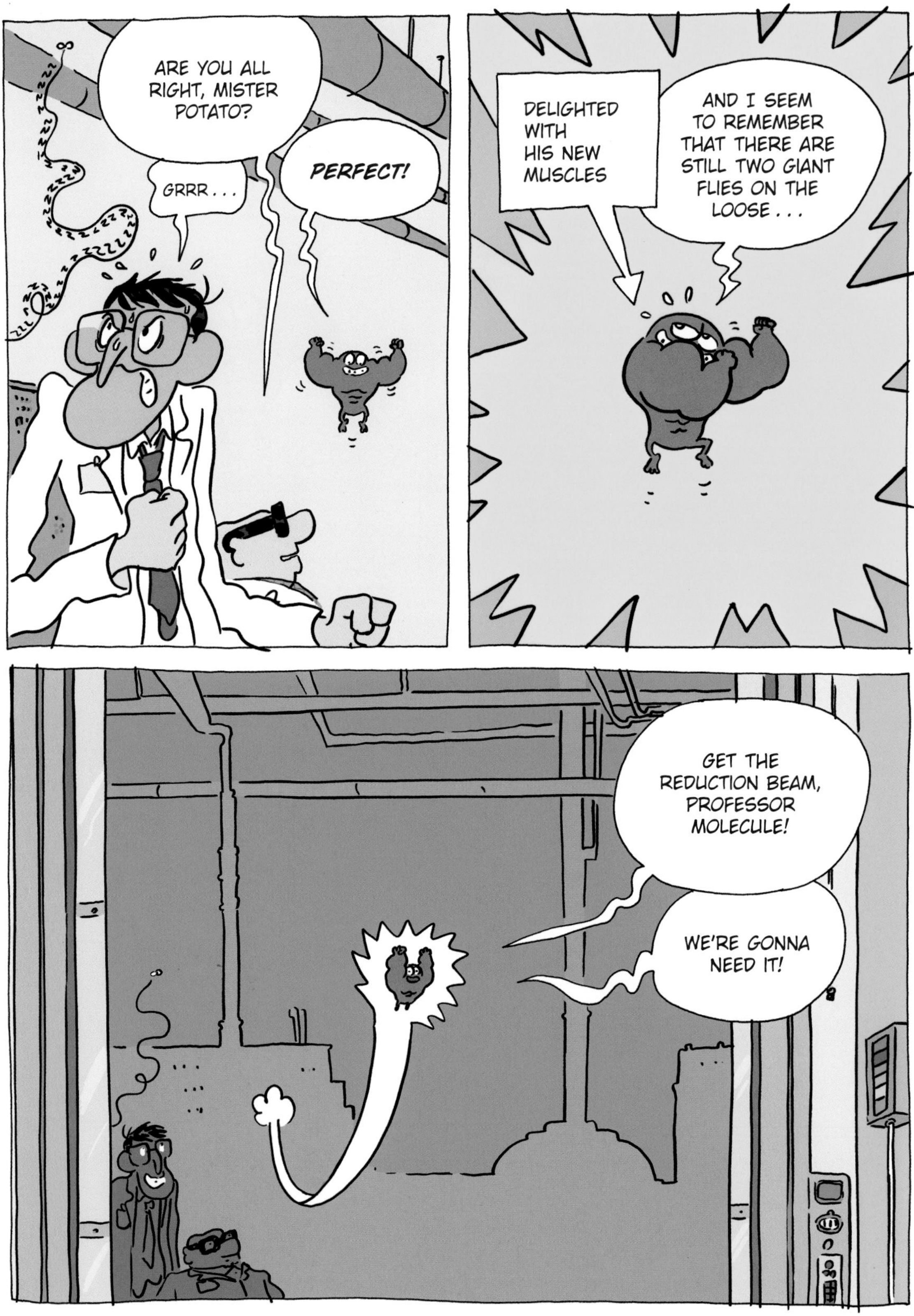

ARE YOU ALL RIGHT, MISTER POTATO?
GRRR . . .
PERFECT!
DELIGHTED WITH HIS NEW MUSCLES
AND I SEEM TO REMEMBER THAT THERE ARE STILL TWO GIANT FLIES ON THE LOOSE . . .
GET THE REDUCTION BEAM, PROFESSOR MOLECULE!
WE'RE GONNA NEED IT!

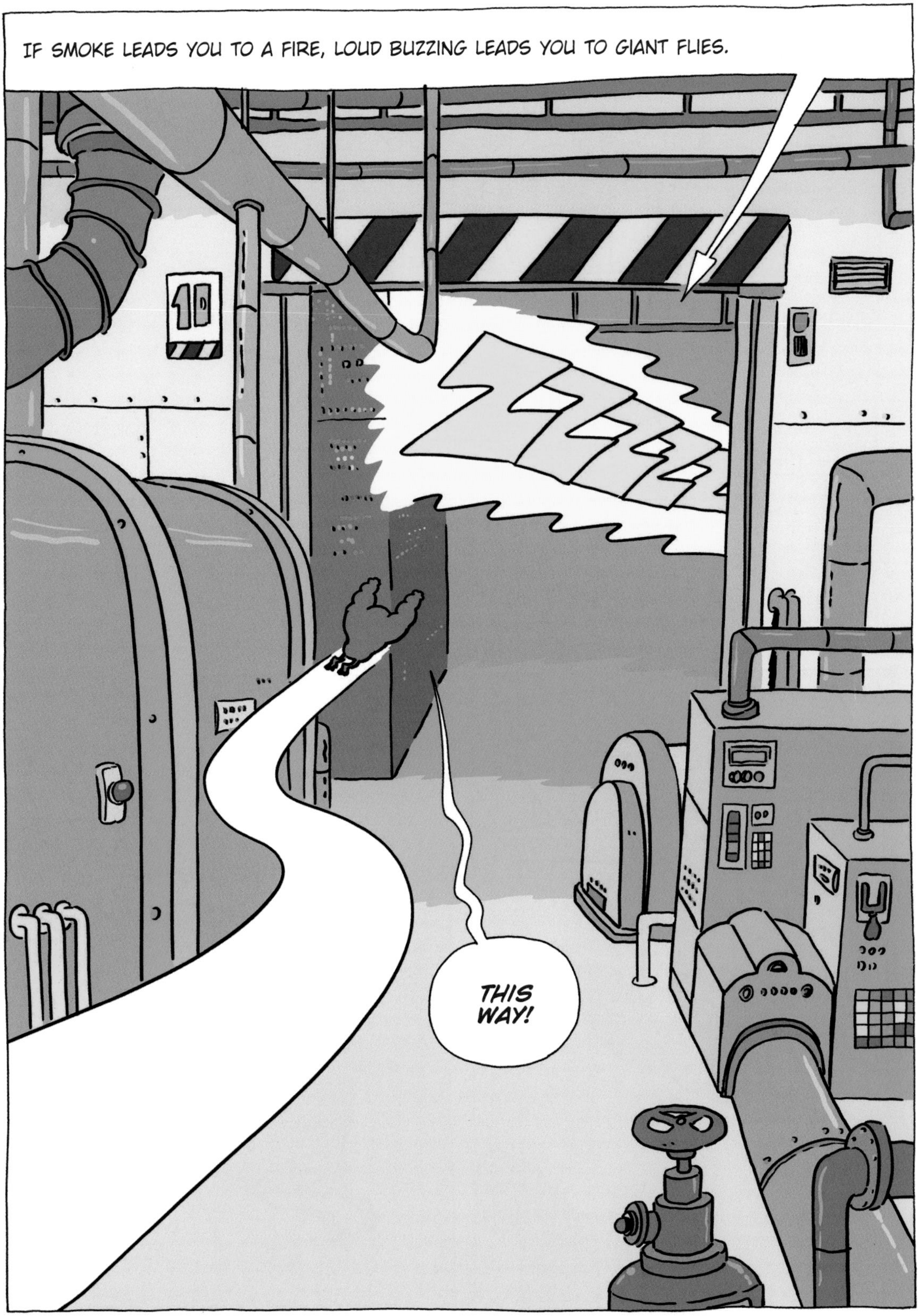
IF SMOKE LEADS YOU TO A FIRE, LOUD BUZZING LEADS YOU TO GIANT FLIES.
THIS WAY!

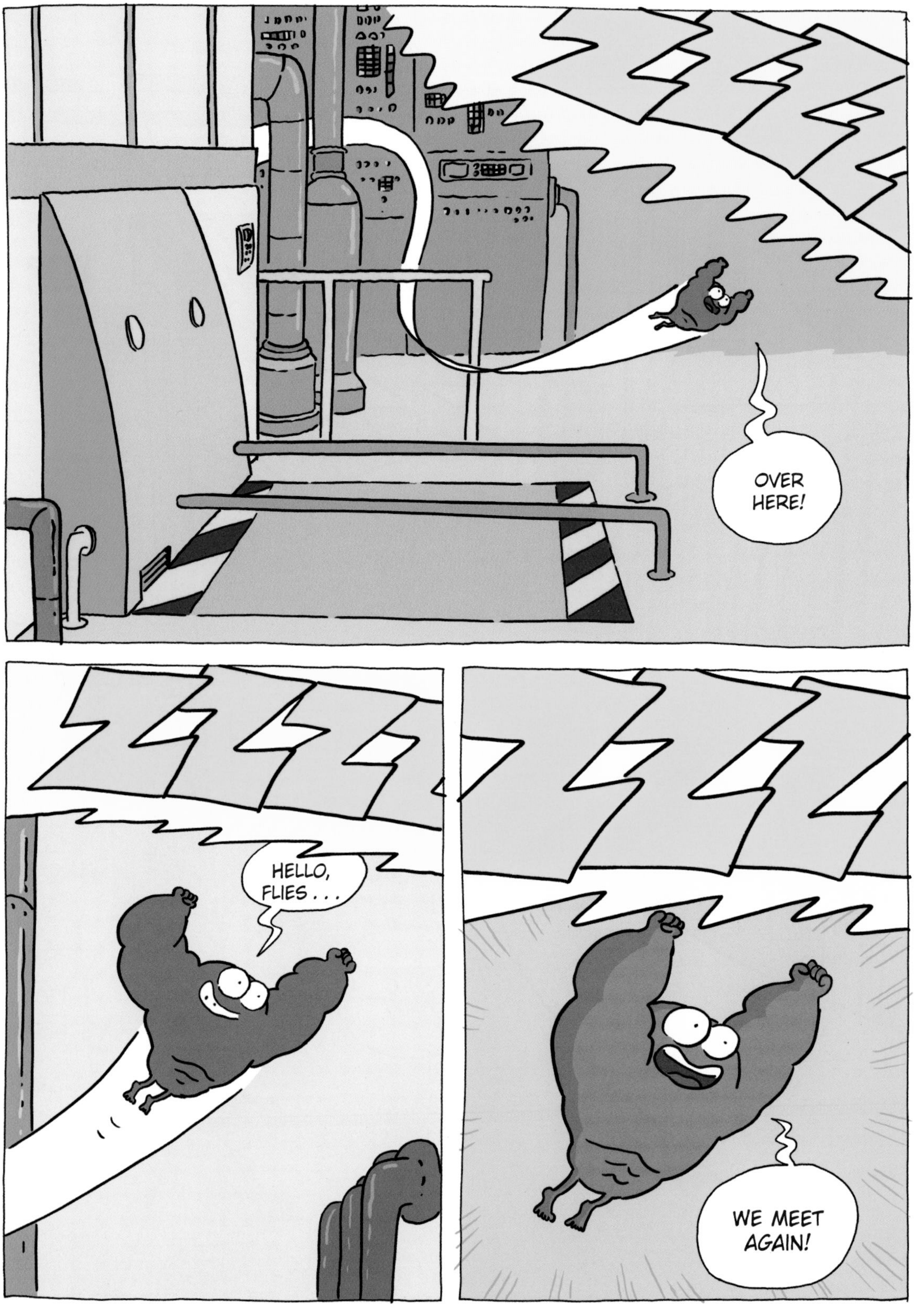
OVER HERE!
HELLO, FLIES . . .
WE MEET AGAIN!

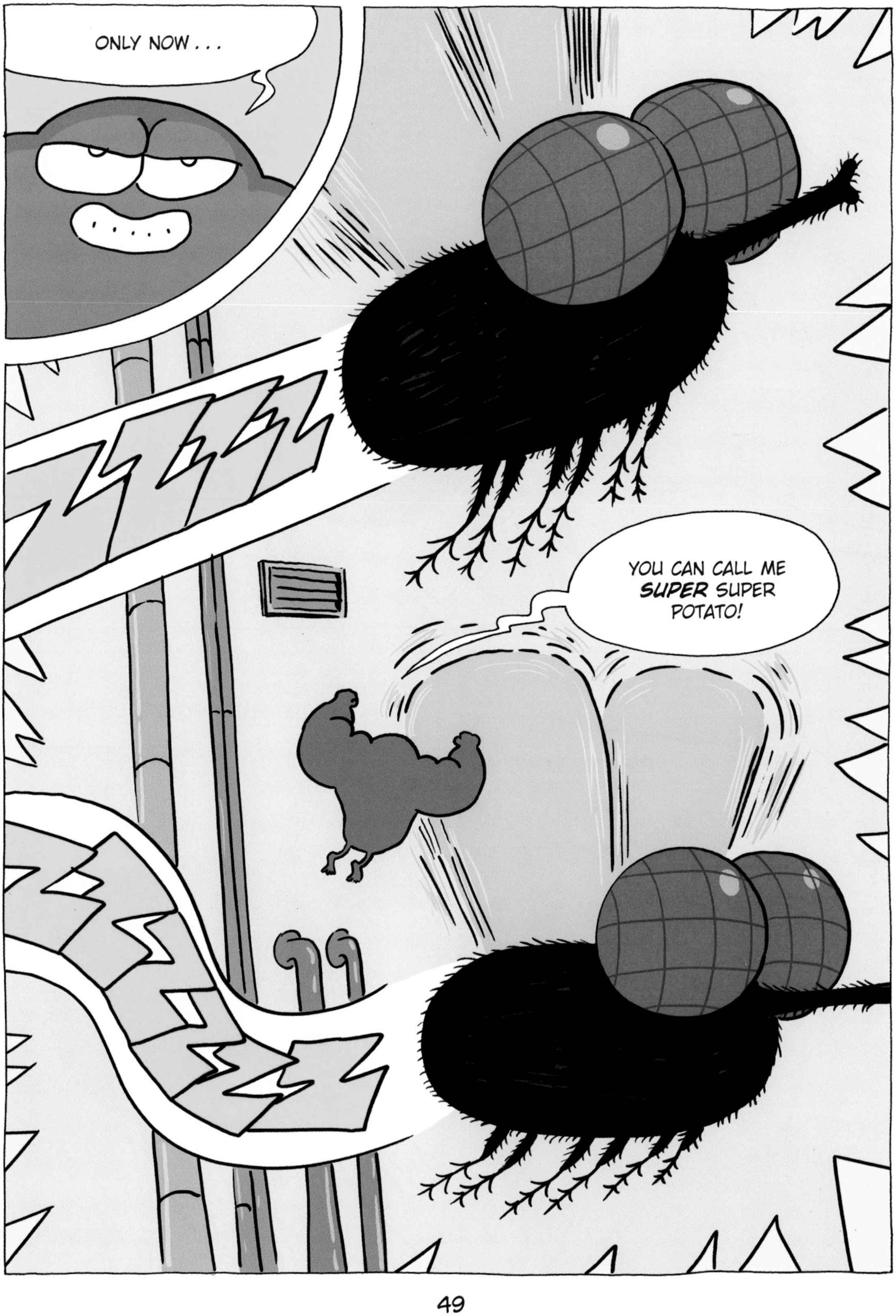
ONLY NOW . . .
YOU CAN CALL ME **SUPER** SUPER POTATO!

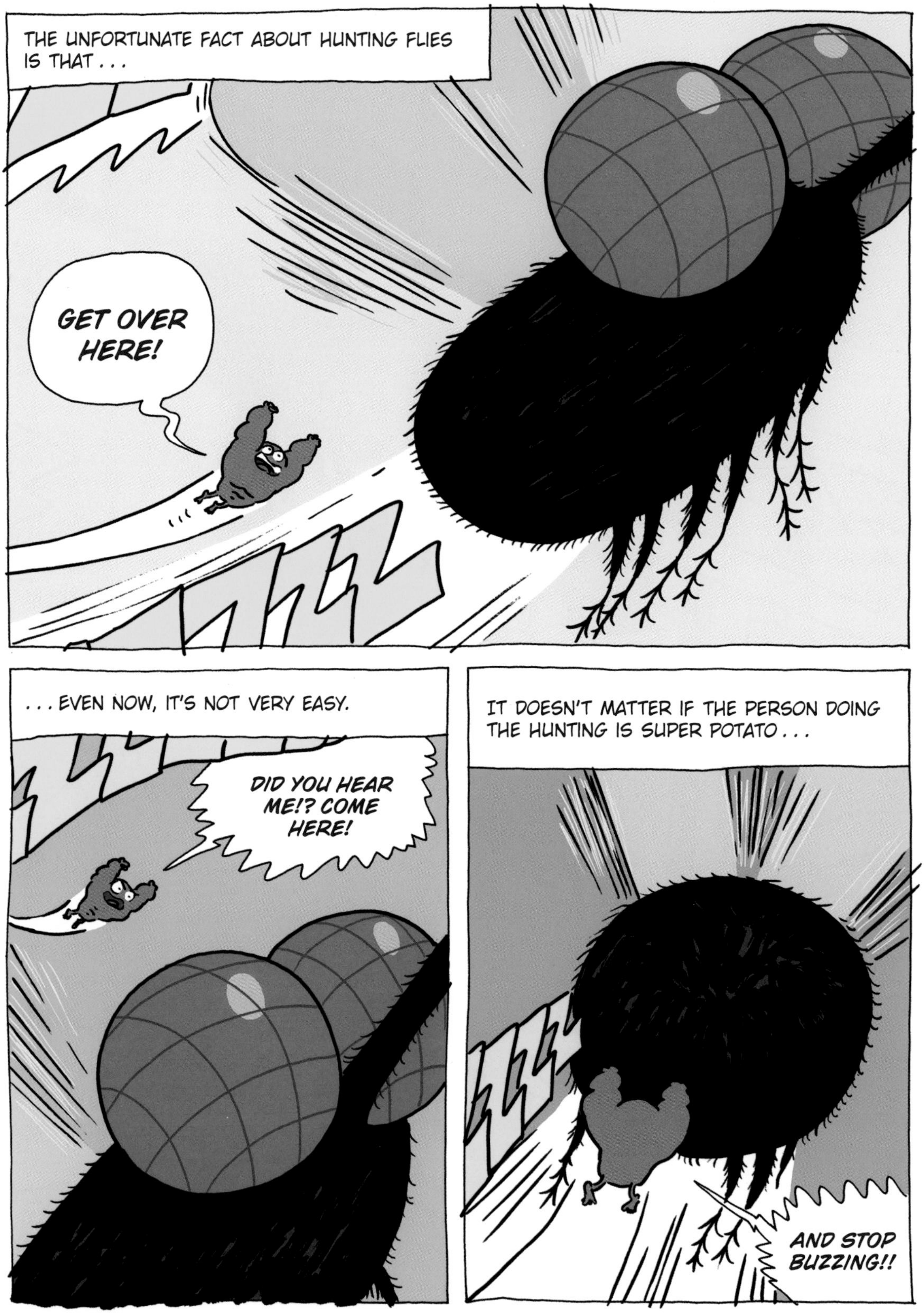
THE UNFORTUNATE FACT ABOUT HUNTING FLIES IS THAT . . .
GET OVER HERE!
. . . EVEN NOW, IT'S NOT VERY EASY.
DID YOU HEAR ME!? COME HERE!
IT DOESN'T MATTER IF THE PERSON DOING THE HUNTING IS SUPER POTATO . . .
AND STOP BUZZING!!

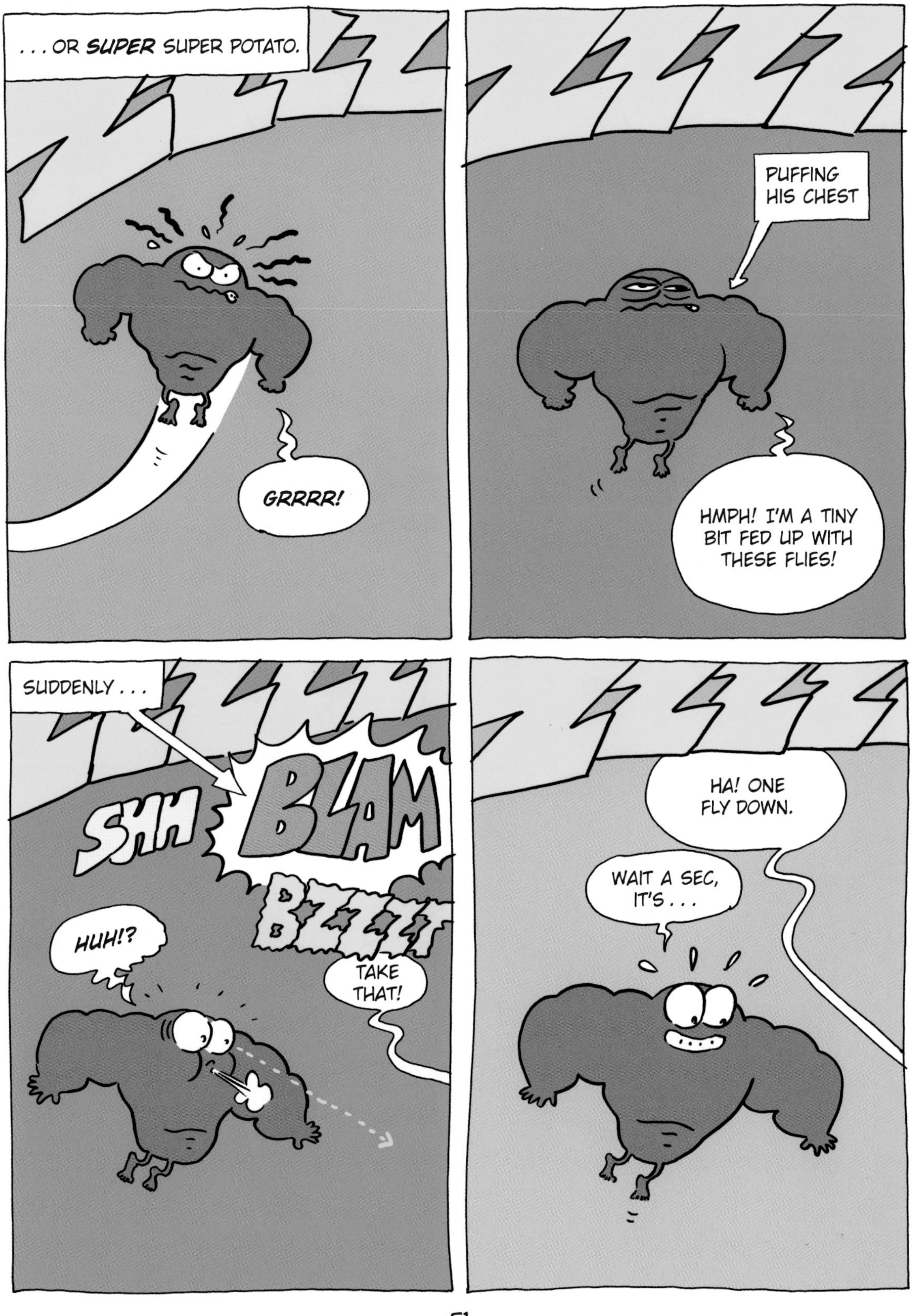
. . . OR **SUPER** SUPER POTATO.
GRRRR!
PUFFING HIS CHEST
HMPH! I'M A TINY BIT FED UP WITH THESE FLIES!
SUDDENLY . . .
SHH
BLAM
BZZZT
HUH!?
TAKE THAT!
HA! ONE FLY DOWN.
WAIT A SEC, IT'S . . .

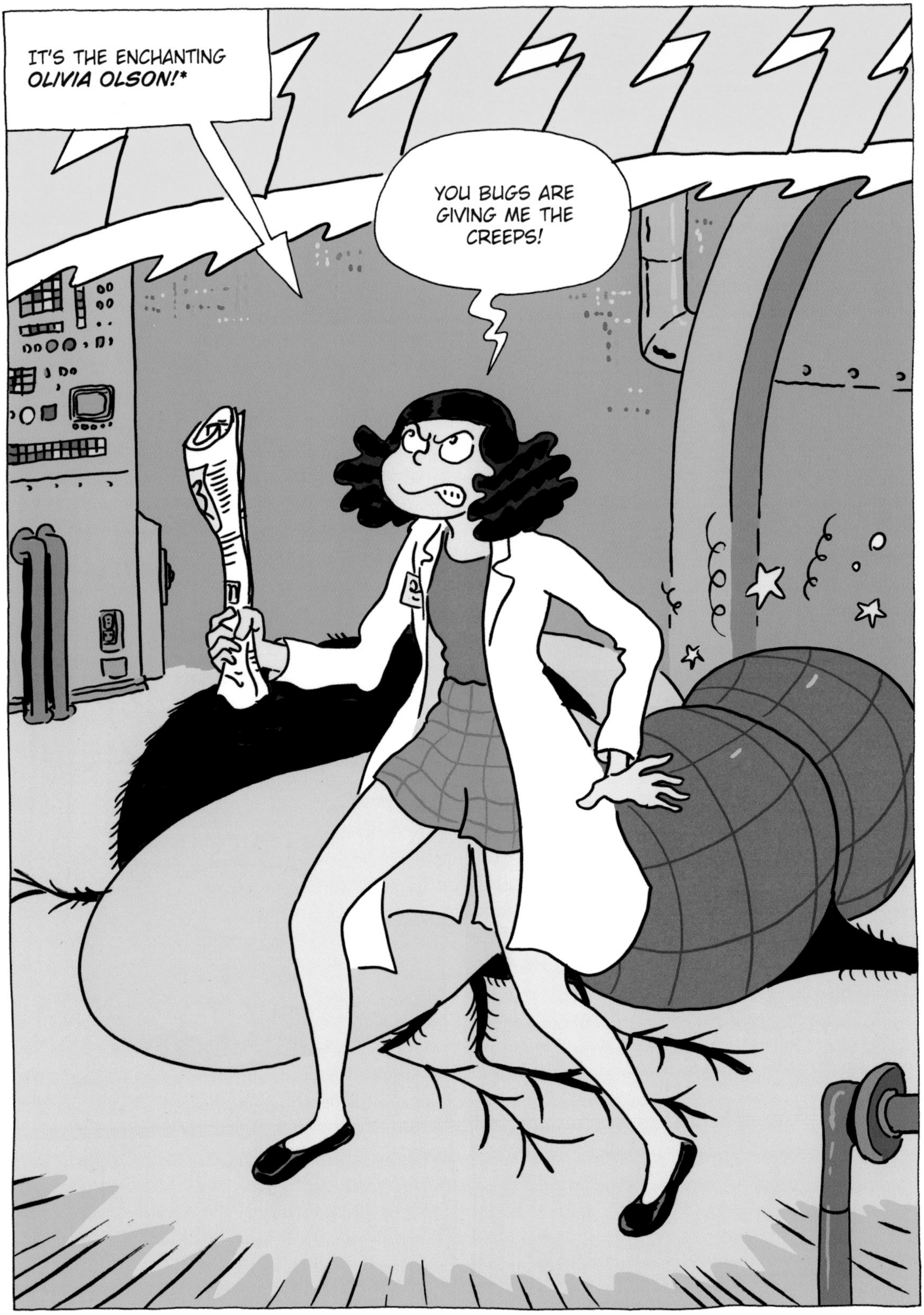
IT'S THE ENCHANTING OLIVIA OLSON!*
YOU BUGS ARE GIVING ME THE CREEPS!

*IF YOU'VE READ ***SUPER POTATO'S MEGA TIME-TRAVEL ADVENTURE*** AND ***SUPER POTATO AND THE MUTANT ANIMAL MAYHEM***, YOU KNOW THAT SUPER POTATO HAS A LITTLE CRUSH ON HER.

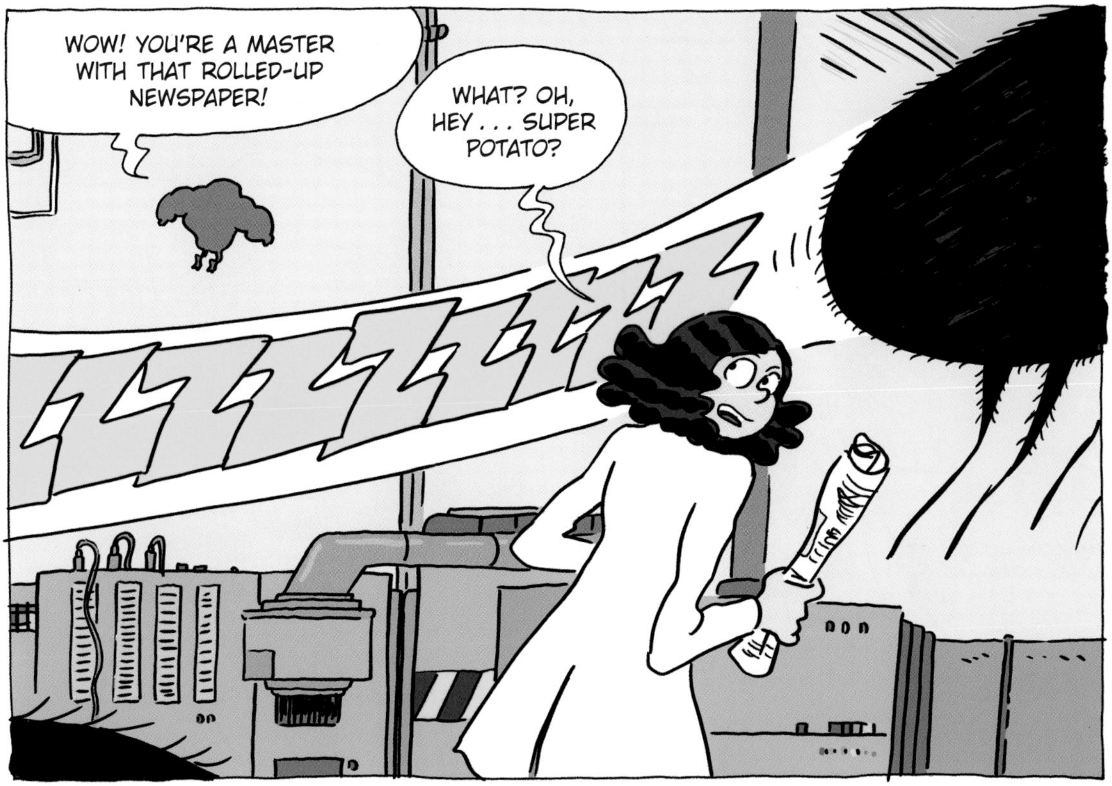
WOW! YOU'RE A MASTER WITH THAT ROLLED-UP NEWSPAPER!
WHAT? OH, HEY . . . SUPER POTATO?

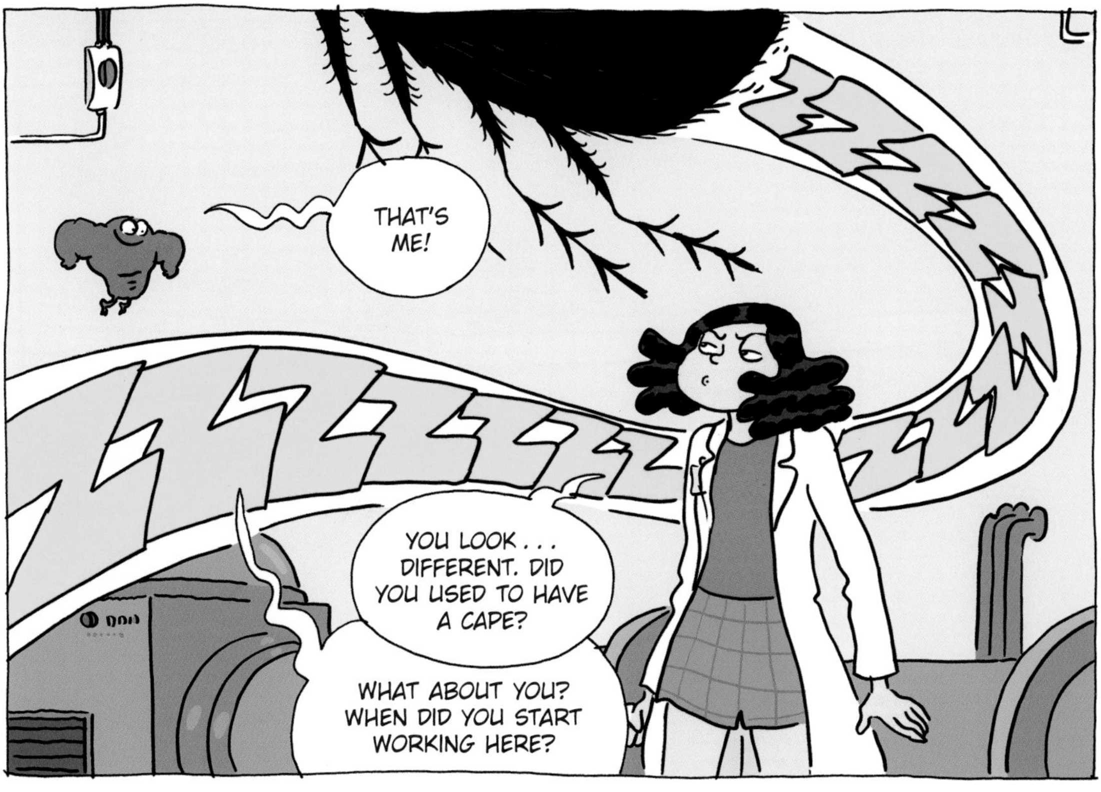
THAT'S ME!
YOU LOOK . . . DIFFERENT. DID YOU USED TO HAVE A CAPE?
WHAT ABOUT YOU? WHEN DID YOU START WORKING HERE?

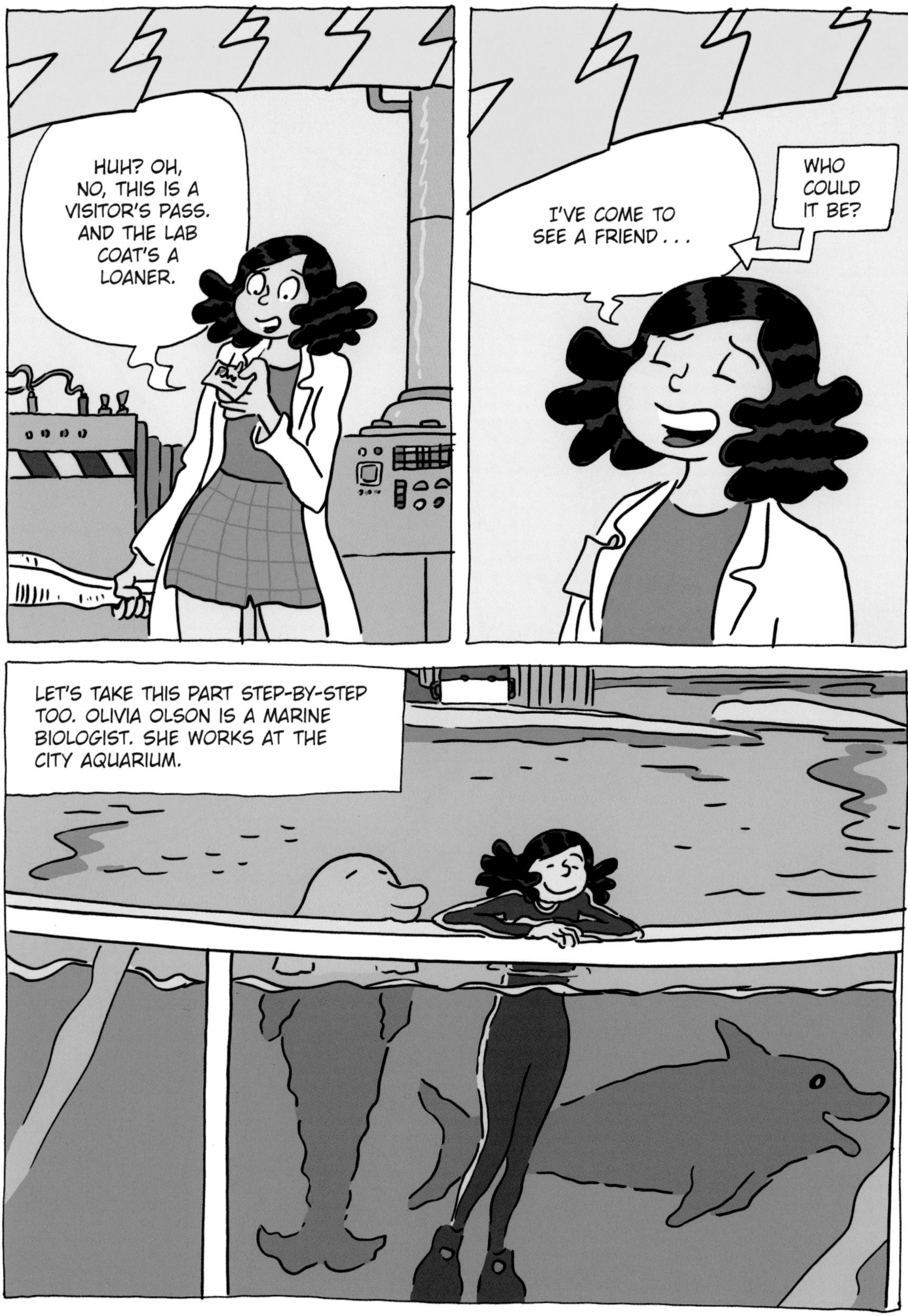
HUH? OH, NO, THIS IS A VISITOR'S PASS. AND THE LAB COAT'S A LOANER.
I'VE COME TO SEE A FRIEND . . .
WHO COULD IT BE?
LET'S TAKE THIS PART STEP-BY-STEP TOO. OLIVIA OLSON IS A MARINE BIOLOGIST. SHE WORKS AT THE CITY AQUARIUM.

SHE'S VISITING THE CORTEX CENTER FOR ULTRA-ADVANCED RESEARCH ALONGSIDE GLADYS, THE SMARTEST DOLPHIN IN THE AQUARIUM. IN THE WHOLE WORLD, PROBABLY.

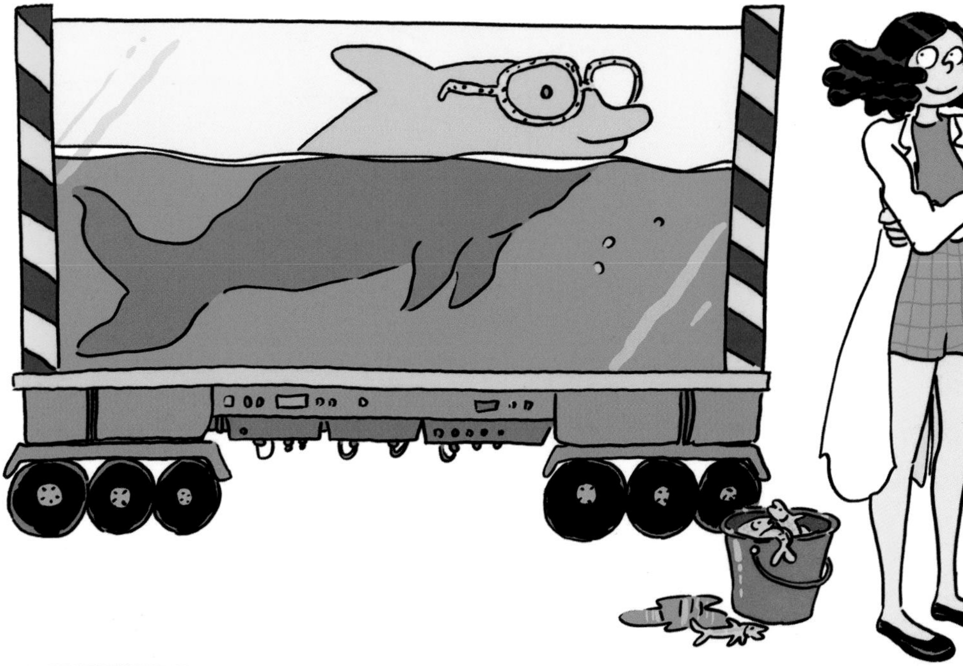

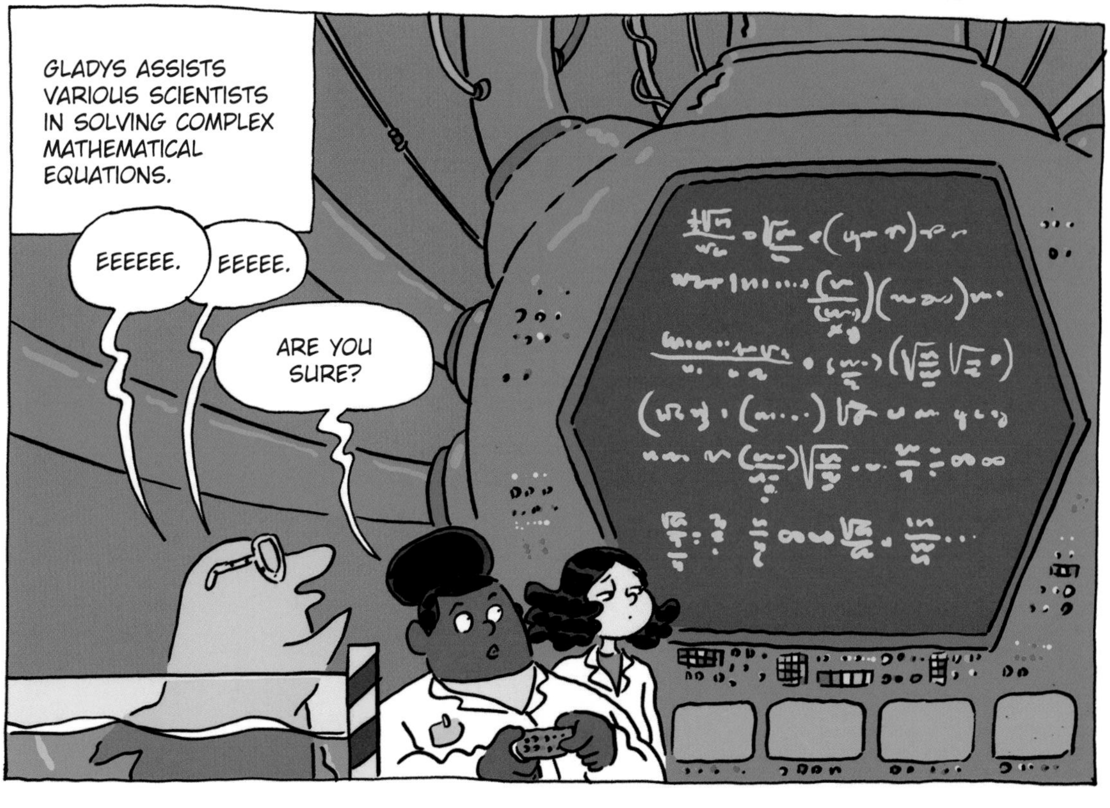
GLADYS ASSISTS VARIOUS SCIENTISTS IN SOLVING COMPLEX MATHEMATICAL EQUATIONS.
EEEEEE.
EEEEE.
ARE YOU SURE?

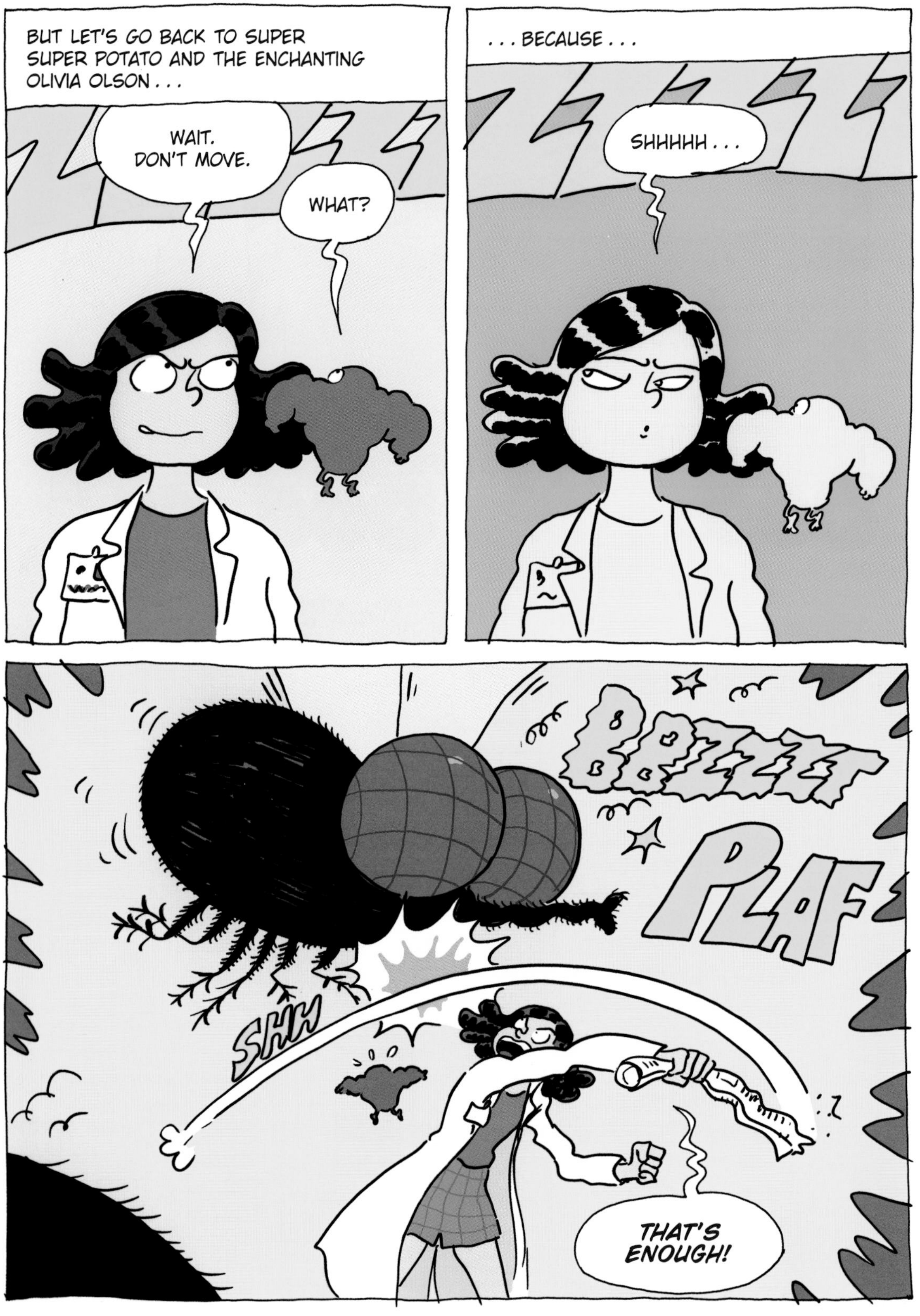
BUT LET'S GO BACK TO SUPER SUPER POTATO AND THE ENCHANTING OLIVIA OLSON . . .
WAIT. DON'T MOVE.
WHAT?
. . . BECAUSE . . .
SHHHHH . . .
BBZZZT
PLAF
SHH
THAT'S ENOUGH!

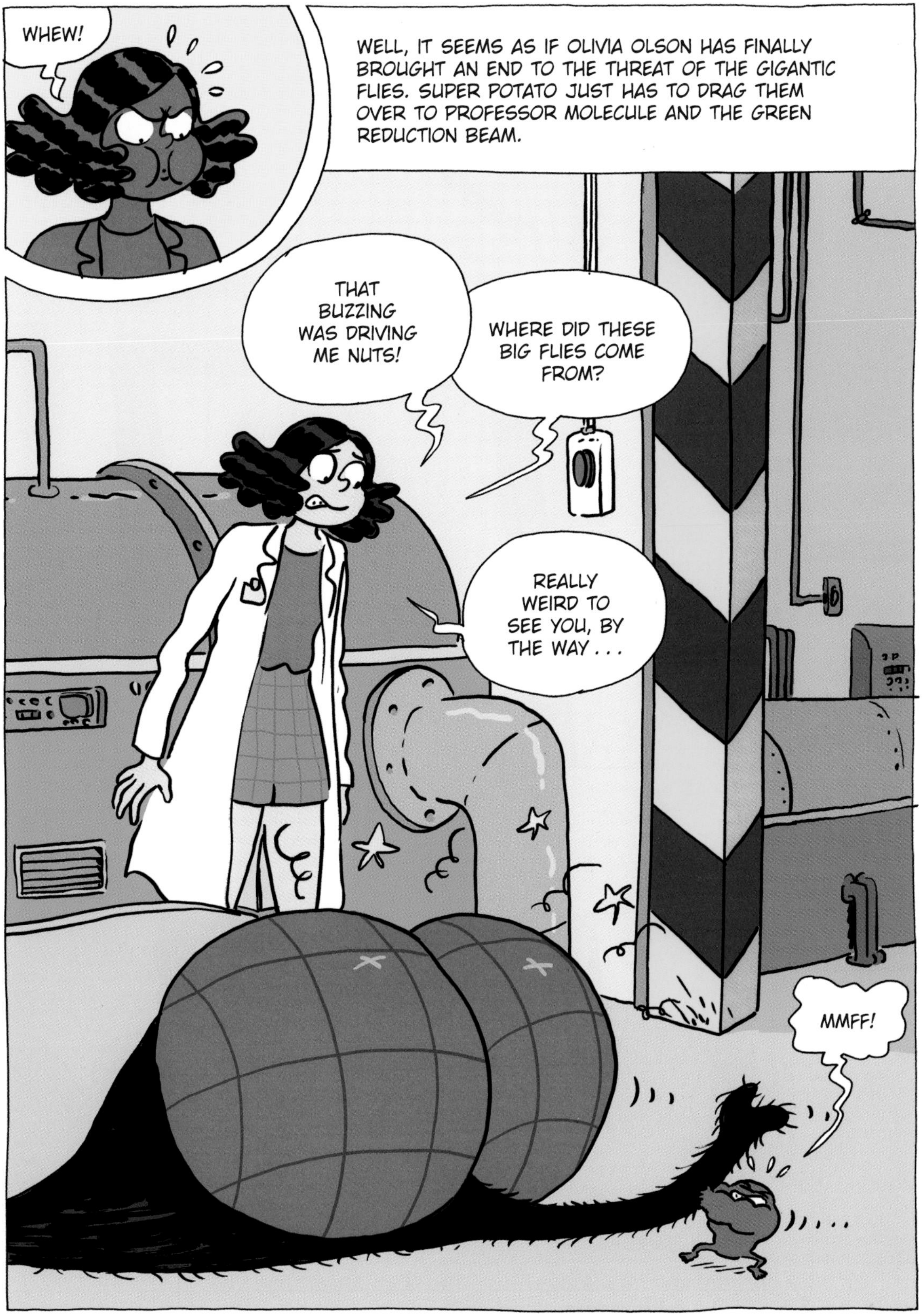
WHEW!
WELL, IT SEEMS AS IF OLIVIA OLSON HAS FINALLY BROUGHT AN END TO THE THREAT OF THE GIGANTIC FLIES. SUPER POTATO JUST HAS TO DRAG THEM OVER TO PROFESSOR MOLECULE AND THE GREEN REDUCTION BEAM.
THAT BUZZING WAS DRIVING ME NUTS!
WHERE DID THESE BIG FLIES COME FROM?
REALLY WEIRD TO SEE YOU, BY THE WAY . . .
MMFF!

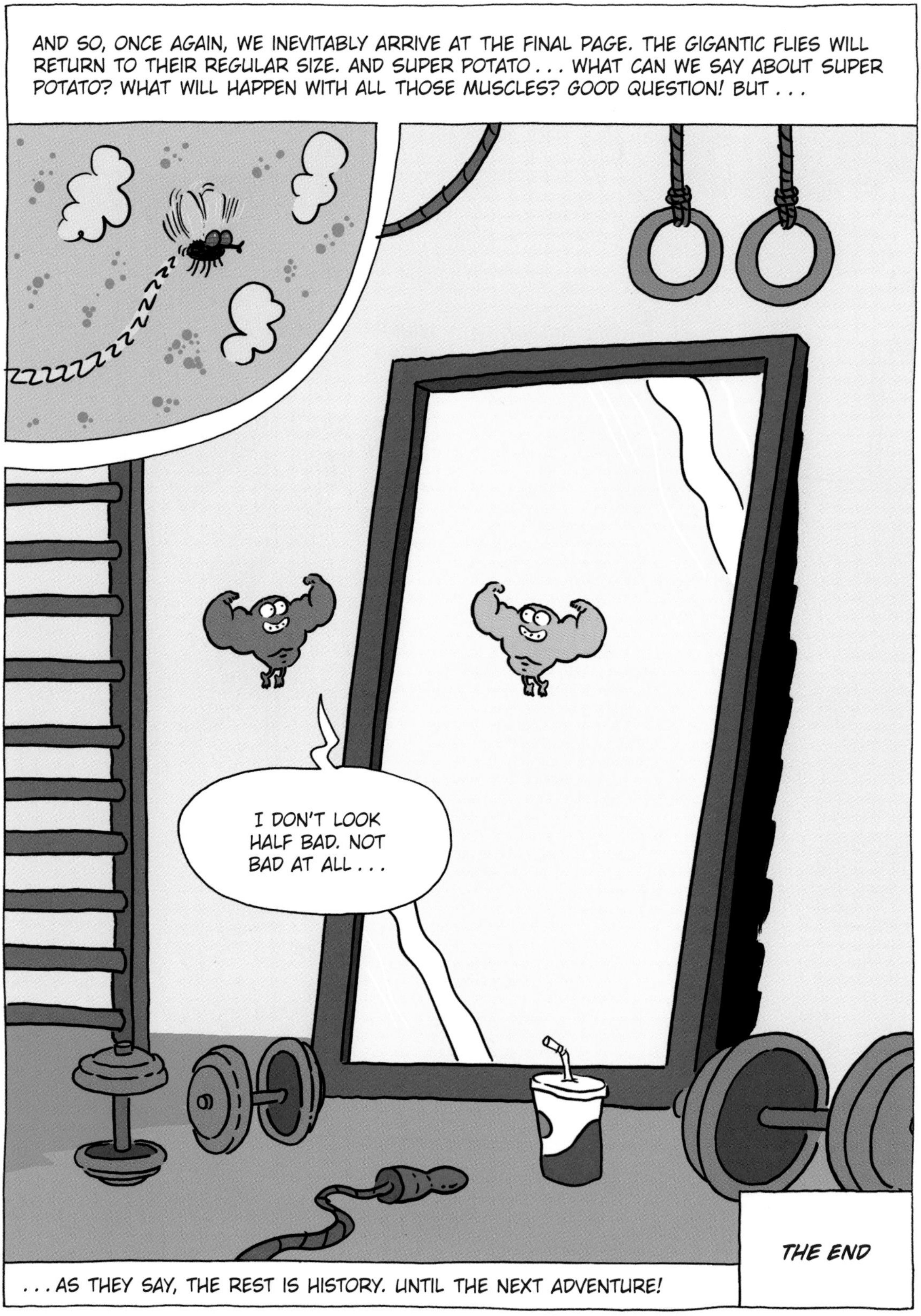
AND SO, ONCE AGAIN, WE INEVITABLY ARRIVE AT THE FINAL PAGE. THE GIGANTIC FLIES WILL RETURN TO THEIR REGULAR SIZE. AND SUPER POTATO . . . WHAT CAN WE SAY ABOUT SUPER POTATO? WHAT WILL HAPPEN WITH ALL THOSE MUSCLES? GOOD QUESTION! BUT . . .
ZZZZZZZZZZZZZZZZZ
I DON'T LOOK HALF BAD. NOT BAD AT ALL . . .
. . . AS THEY SAY, THE REST IS HISTORY. UNTIL THE NEXT ADVENTURE!
THE END

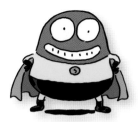

For more hilarious tales of Super Potato, check out . . .

SUPER POTATO
#1 THE EPIC ORIGIN OF SUPER POTATO
Artur Laperla

SUPER POTATO
#2 SUPER POTATO'S GALACTIC BREAKOUT
Artur Laperla

SUPER POTATO
#3 SUPER POTATO'S MEGA TIME-TRAVEL ADVENTURE
Artur Laperla

SUPER POTATO
#4 SUPER POTATO AND THE MUTANT ANIMAL MAYHEM
Artur Laperla

SUPER POTATO
#5 SUPER POTATO AND THE CASTLE OF ROBOTS
Artur Laperla

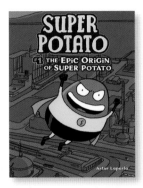

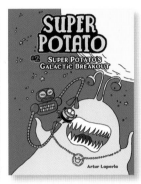

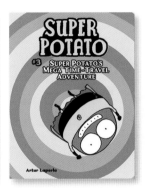

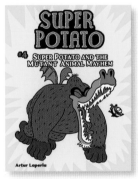

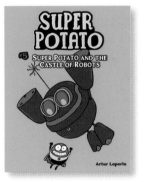

AND TURN THE PAGE FOR A PREVIEW OF OUR HERO'S NEXT GREAT ADVENTURE . . .

SUPER POTATO #7

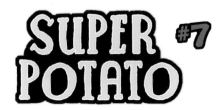

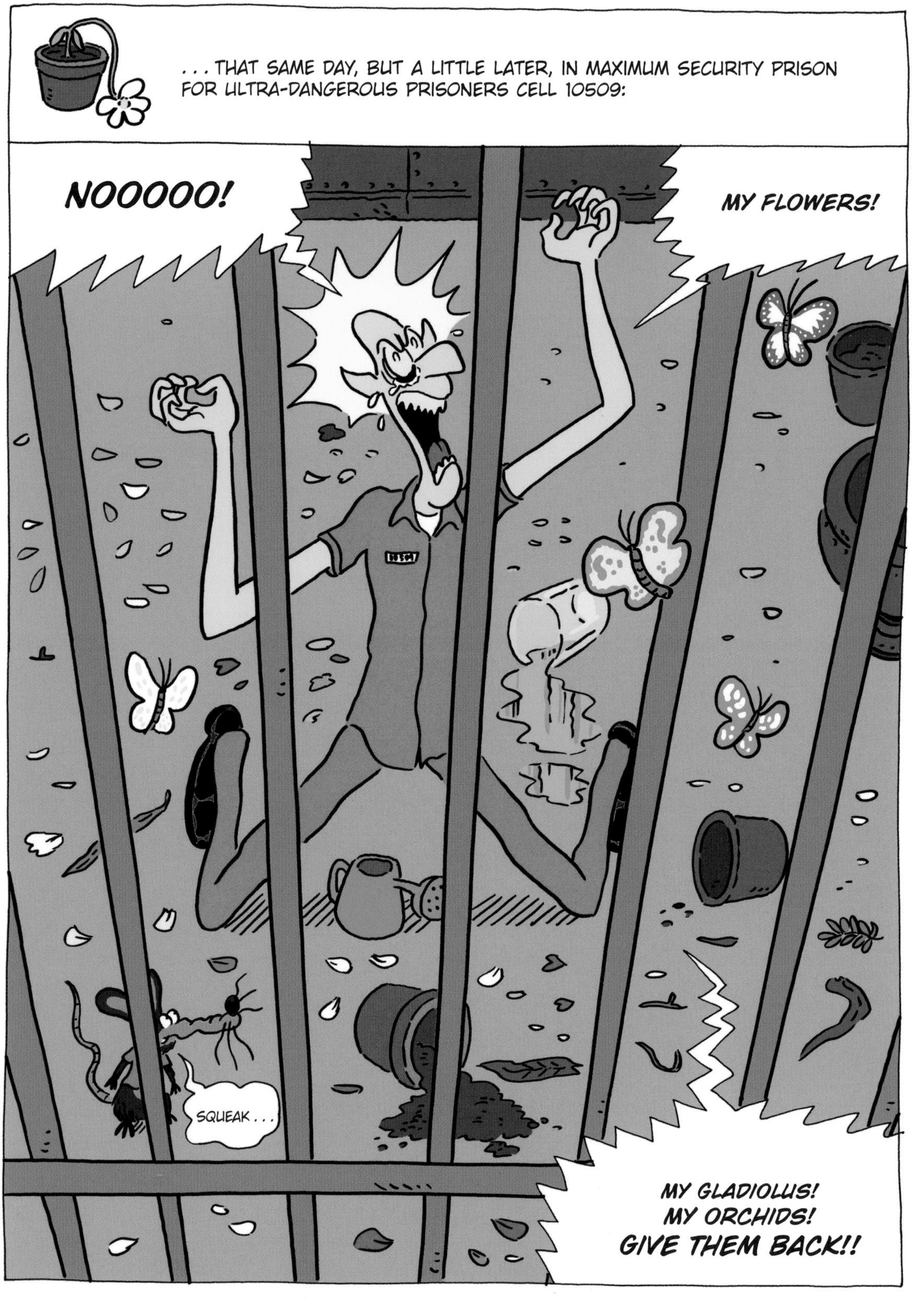

. . . THAT SAME DAY, BUT A LITTLE LATER, IN MAXIMUM SECURITY PRISON FOR ULTRA-DANGEROUS PRISONERS CELL 10509:
NOOOOO!
MY FLOWERS!
SQUEAK . . .
MY GLADIOLUS!
MY ORCHIDS!
GIVE THEM BACK!!

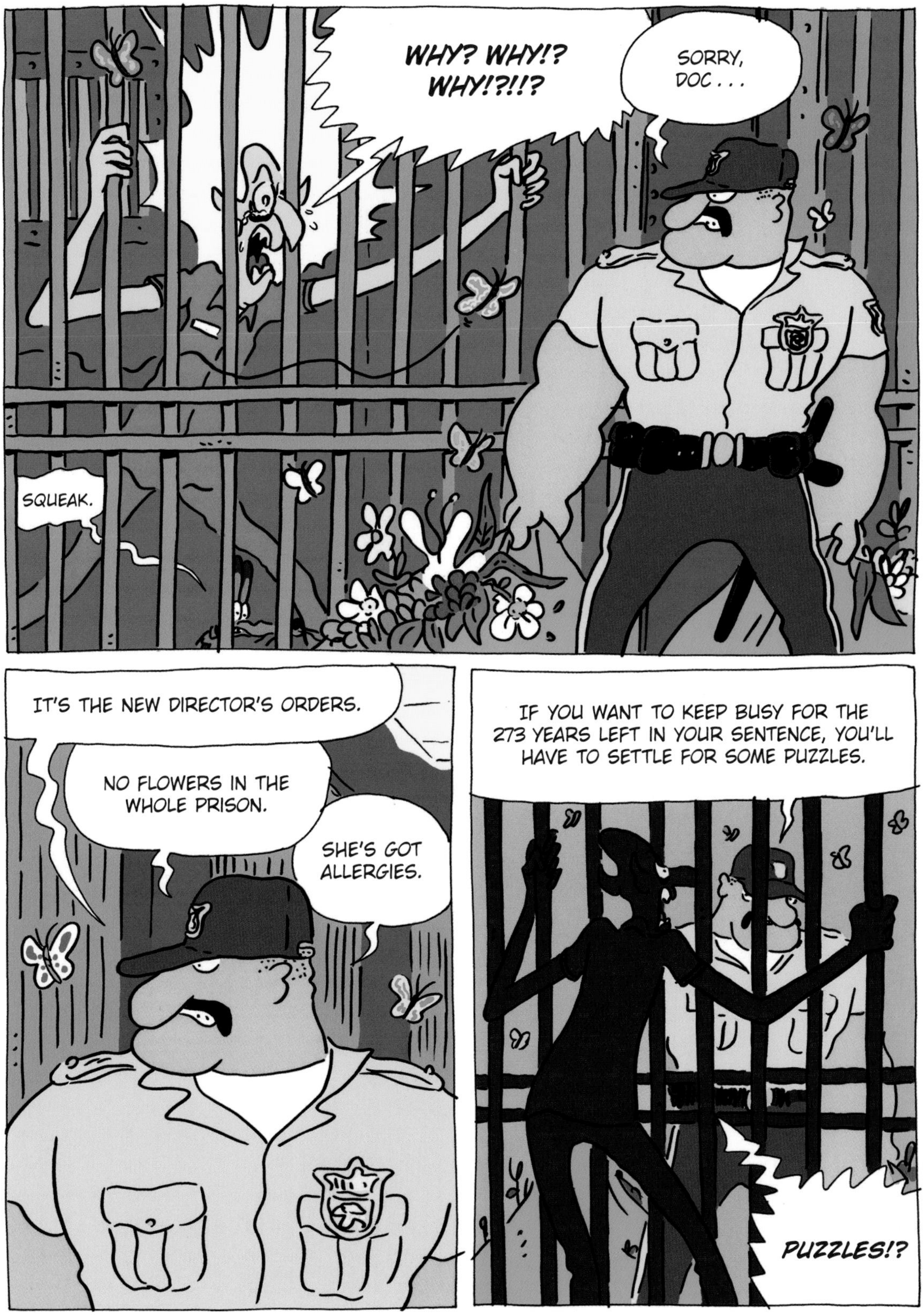
WHY? WHY!? WHY!?!!?
SORRY, DOC . . .
SQUEAK.
IT'S THE NEW DIRECTOR'S ORDERS.
NO FLOWERS IN THE WHOLE PRISON.
SHE'S GOT ALLERGIES.
IF YOU WANT TO KEEP BUSY FOR THE 273 YEARS LEFT IN YOUR SENTENCE, YOU'LL HAVE TO SETTLE FOR SOME PUZZLES.
PUZZLES!?

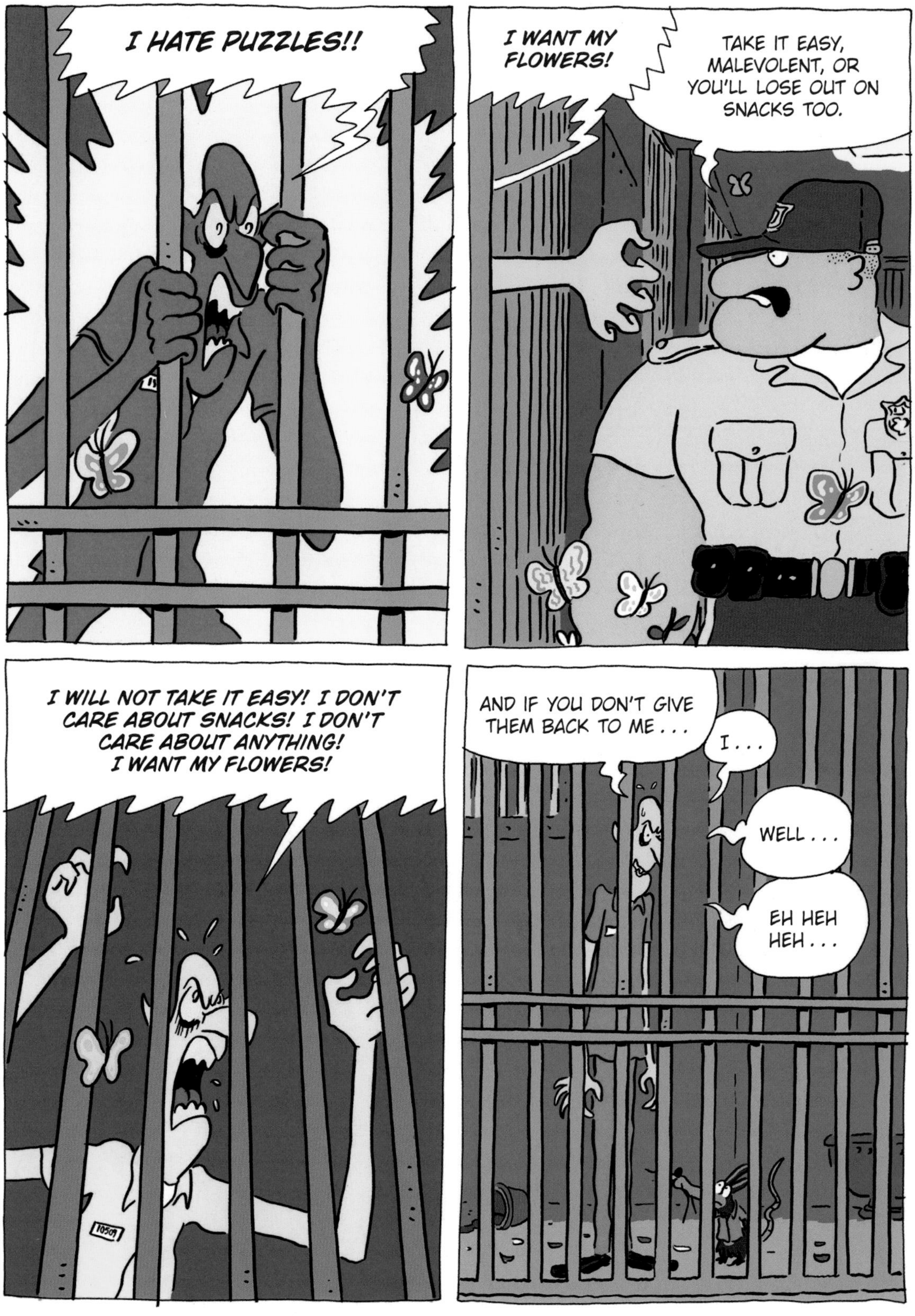
I HATE PUZZLES!!
I WANT MY FLOWERS!
TAKE IT EASY, MALEVOLENT, OR YOU'LL LOSE OUT ON SNACKS TOO.
I WILL NOT TAKE IT EASY! I DON'T CARE ABOUT SNACKS! I DON'T CARE ABOUT ANYTHING! I WANT MY FLOWERS!
AND IF YOU DON'T GIVE THEM BACK TO ME . . .
I . . .
WELL . . .
EH HEH HEH . . .

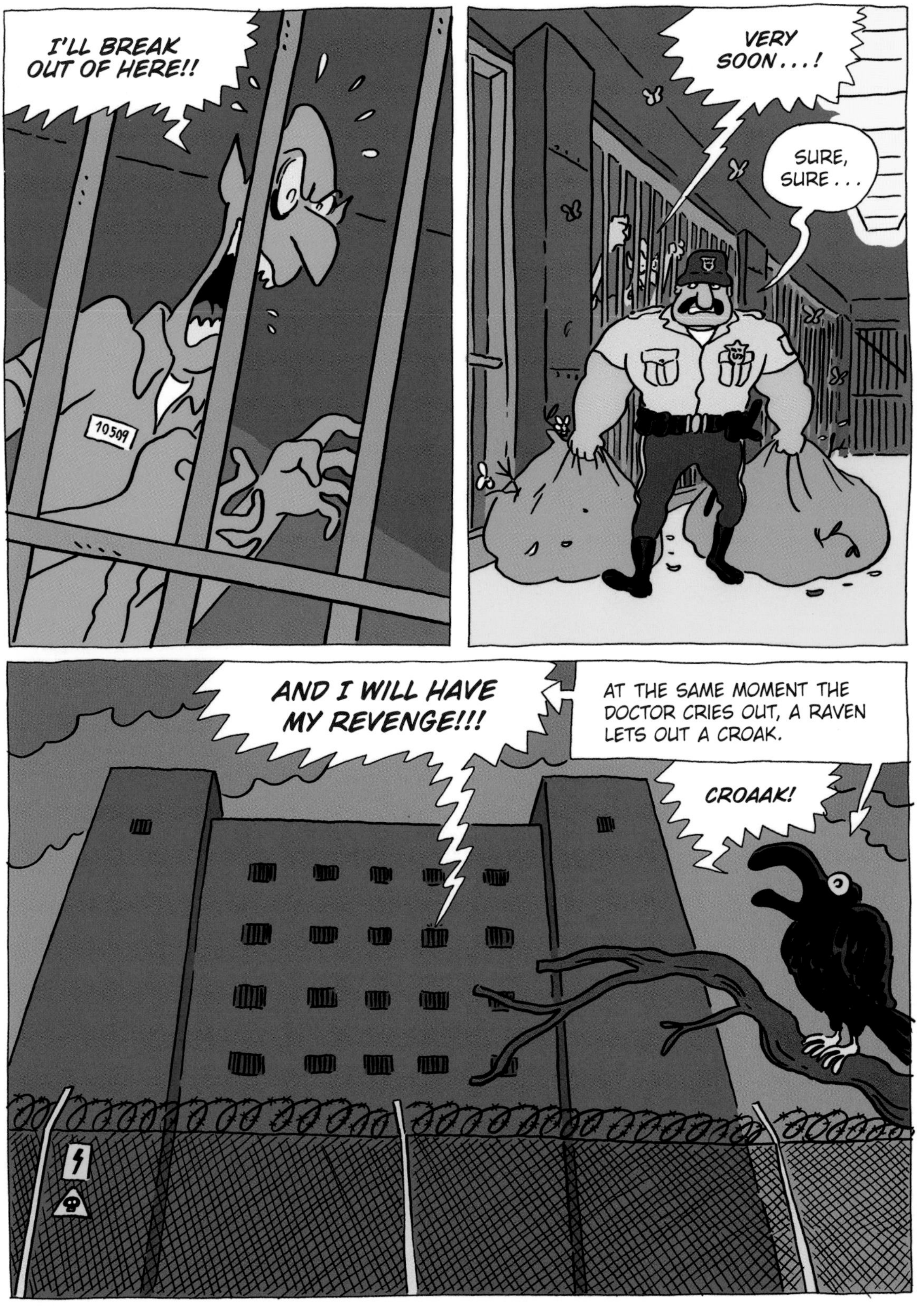
I'LL BREAK OUT OF HERE!!
10509
VERY SOON . . . !
SURE, SURE . . .
AND I WILL HAVE MY REVENGE!!!
AT THE SAME MOMENT THE DOCTOR CRIES OUT, A RAVEN LETS OUT A CROAK.
CROAAK!

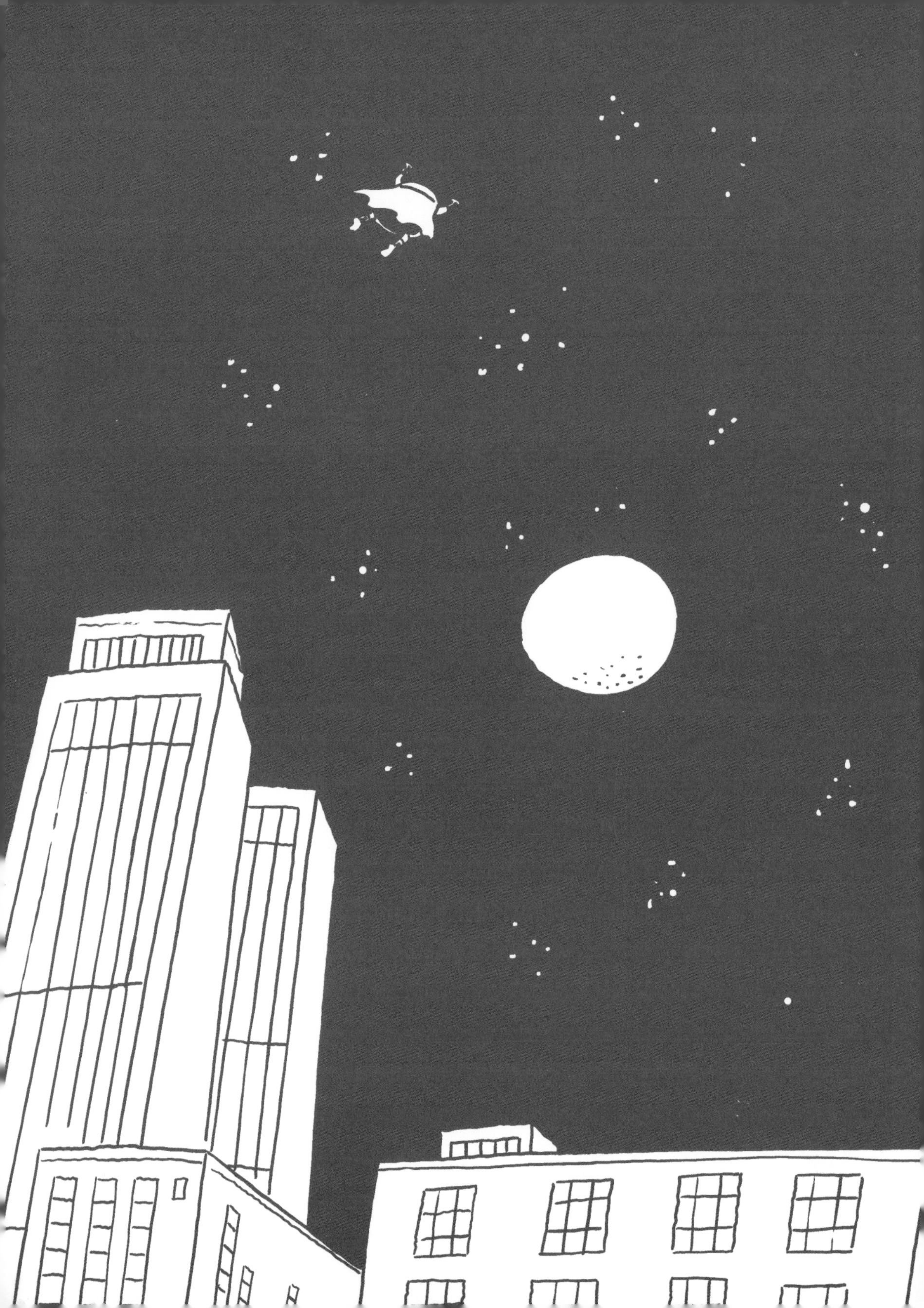